TWICE T[...]

Enid Richemont was born and brought up in Wales. She started writing young, and, at eleven, was crowned Bard of a youth Eisteddfod. On leaving school, she studied at Dublin College of Art and then wrote short stories for magazines before starting her own design business, producing play equipment for children. She began writing children's stories to entertain her son and daughter and their friends and, in 1989, Walker Books published her first novel, *The Time Tree*. This has since been followed by a number of books for young readers, *The Glass Bird, The Magic Skateboard, Kachunka!* and *Gemma and the Beetle People*, as well as a story for older readers, *The Game*. Enid Richemont lives in London.

Books by the same author

The Game
My Mother's Daughter
The Time Tree
Wolfsong

For younger readers

Gemma and the Beetle People
The Glass Bird
Kachunka!
The Magic Skateboard

TWICE TIMES DANGER

ENID RICHEMONT

WALKER BOOKS
AND SUBSIDIARIES
LONDON · BOSTON · SYDNEY

First published 1995 by Walker Books Ltd
87 Vauxhall Walk, London SE11 5HJ

This edition published 1995

2 4 6 8 10 9 7 5 3 1

Text © 1995 Enid Richemont
Cover illustration © 1995 Julie Douglas

This book has been typeset in Sabon.

Printed in England

British Library Cataloguing in Publication Data
A catalogue record for this book is available from
the British Library.

ISBN 0-7445-4347-9

*For
Anne Carter,
with love*

CHAPTER ONE

They'd already put up a poster. Becca saw it on her way out of the police station with Mum. It was like a stage prop, she thought. It couldn't be real.

HAVE YOU SEEN THIS GIRL? the words said.

And there was Daisie's round, funny face, blown up and slightly blurred, with that cheese-smile she put on for school photographs, her long hair scraped back behind a headband.

MISSING FROM HOME. DAISIE TREVELYAN. AGED ELEVEN.

Would they give it to her as a souvenir? wondered Becca.

When they'd sorted things out. When they'd found her.

For nothing really bad could have happened, she kept telling herself. Not to Daisie Trevelyan. Not Daisie. Things happened to people in newspapers, people on the telly. Not real people. Not people you knew.

Not your best friend.

Mum squeezed Becca's hand. "You did well," she said.

Becca gulped. *What did I do?* she thought. *Nothing much. Told that police lady where we went, where we played, about Dita. (And what was the point of that? She didn't believe me.)* Becca grinned. *Wait till they pick her up. That'll give them a shock.*

Mum made tea when they got back, scraping Marmite over thin slices of toast, opening a pack of cheeses and arranging Becca's favourite biscuits in a flower pattern. "Eat something," she said, offering things to Becca as if she were a guest. "You'll feel better if you eat." But even the warm, milky tea seemed difficult to swallow.

Becca picked up her mug and took it into the garden, just to get away from Mum's worried face. *Nothing is going to happen to me,* she thought irritably. Just because one girl went missing, it didn't mean that there was some maniac out there, doing people in.

Did it?

"Don't go wandering off," called Mum anxiously.

So Becca stayed in the garden, hunched behind the apple tree, where Mum could just see her from the kitchen window. She felt empty. She felt bored. There was nothing to do. There was nothing she wanted to do. How could you read or watch telly when your best friend was missing?

Maybe Daisie'd gone off somewhere. She was always doing crazy things.

Maybe she was dead. Murdered.

No more Daisie...

But how could someone like Daisie just stop? That was too scary to think about.

And Becca needed to think, to try to work it all out, but not at home, in the garden, with Mum fussing, and the possibility of the two old ladies coming back early from their coach trip. She pulled a face. *"Emmets,"* she muttered (using the local rude word for tourists). She could just *hear* them gasping, *Ooh!* and, *Aah!* and, *Aren't these things dreadful?* As if bad things never happened where they came from.

And Becca needed to walk. By herself. Down the long lane to the beach, or up to their seal-watching hide on the cliffs.

But Mum was jumpy. "Make sure you go out in a group," she kept saying. "There's safety in numbers."

But Becca didn't want people.

Becca wanted Daisie.

They'd been best friends for nearly two years. Then that girl Dita had turned up. Becca wished *she'd* disappeared instead of Daisie.

From the moment they'd met her, it had

9

been like living inside some fantastic story.

Only it wasn't Becca's story. It was theirs.

Daisie's.

And Perdita's.

CHAPTER
TWO

Things had been slightly odd all summer.

There had been an unease between Daisie and Becca – nothing they could put a name to, more like a sickening for something, like a suspicion of a sore throat, like the ghost of a headache that wasn't really there.

True, they were going on to different schools, but they'd talked about that. After all, they still lived only a few streets apart. They could still muck around together, go to the beach, see friends – things you did out of school anyway.

But there was the day that Becca put on her new uniform.

"You look like a right prat," sniffed Daisie.

"I don't *want* to go to a girls' school," said Becca, hurt.

"Then don't," said Daisie.

"It's OK for you," grumbled Becca. "Your

11

mum lets you do anything."

Then Daisie'd flushed pink. "You lot think you're so special!"

And even that afternoon on the beach, when it all began, they'd been working up to a quarrel. Daisie's dog, Drac, seemed to pick up their mood, pestering them for sticks and barking at nothing.

The girls sniped at each other.

"But I saw you."

"Well, you couldn't have," said Daisie. "I was helping Mum."

"You were with this sexy blonde woman," insisted Becca. "In the cake shop. I saw you."

"I wasn't!"

"And I said 'Hi!' and you just looked at me as if you didn't know me."

"You're bananas," said Daisie. She picked up a piece of driftwood and threw it for Drac. The small, spiky-haired mongrel scuttered over the stones and began splashing furiously through shallow waves. They watched his head, like a little black ball, bobbing determinedly towards the target.

"Look out!" shrieked Daisie when he began paddling back. "He's coming for us! We'll be drenched!" And their squabbling stopped.

"Let's climb," Becca said. "Let's go to the other beach." So they ran, their feet crunching over the pebbles, making for the rocks.

Halfway across the point, they stopped to

watch Drac hauling his trophy backwards along the beach, wrestling with it, gnawing, growling, dropping it, sniffing the air, then galloping towards them, picking up their scent.

"Come on!" puffed Daisie. "Quick! Before he gets here!"

They scrambled down the other side, weaving between rock pools, balancing, slithering, then easing themselves round the big flattish beach rocks covered in squelchy cushions of slippery weed. Then they clambered around a shallow point, and stepped on to damp sand.

The little cove lay in an unbroken curve, like a pale gold web spun between two arms of rock. They'd found it at the beginning of the school holidays, on one of their short cuts to the coast path. They'd just looked down and there it was. They couldn't think why they'd never spotted it before.

"I think I know your little cove," Daisie's mum had said afterwards, spreading out a map. "It's here, see? Looks as if you can get to it from the main road now. And those dotted lines – that's a footpath." She picked up the car keys. "Shall we go and see?"

But a short way out of Tregennack, she'd pulled up along a newly-made road. "Some footpath," she'd grumbled, pointing to the sign saying GUINEVERE DEVELOPMENTS. PRIVATE ROAD. "They've been building down there – I remember reading about it. Smugglers Cove,

I think they were calling it – they would! Holiday homes for people with more money than sense. Let's have a look." That was the thing about Daisie's mum – things like PRIVATE signs never bothered her.

So after that, the girls savoured the idea that they might be trespassing, that some warden, some parkie, might come raging out of one of the empty houses, and then they'd have to scramble back over the rocks and run for it.

"There aren't any private beaches in Cornwall," Daisie's mum had told them firmly. "Or if there are, there shouldn't be."

"It's really the estate that's private," said Daisie that afternoon. "There's no notice on the beach."

"Oh, but wouldn't *you* want to make this beach private," argued Becca, "if you lived in one of those posh houses?"

Daisie laughed. "If we could afford one of those," she said, "I wouldn't stay in Cornwall. I'd be off to Florida. Or the south of France."

"Who wants the south of France," drooled Becca, "when they can have a place like this all to themselves?" She looked along the sand: smooth, unbroken, except for the tracks the gulls had made, and the worm casts down at the water's edge. "It's like a desert island," she sighed. "I always feel like the First Man. You know, making the first step."

Daisie grinned. "You can't be the First *Man*, my bird."

"OK, OK, the First Woman, then."

"Watch out! Here comes the First Dog," said Daisie, but Drac walked right past them, as if they weren't there.

Some distance away, he began scratching a hole.

"Oh, no," groaned Daisie. "The First Dog is making the First Poo."

Becca giggled. "People will dig it up," she said, "in thousands of years' time, like dinosaurs' bones, and they'll say, 'Now who made this poo?'"

Daisie frowned. "That's a late twentieth century poo," she said, putting on a deep voice, "made by Dracula, the only vampire dog in Cornwall."

They collapsed into giggles, rolling in the sand. Drac ran up to them, wanting to join in.

"No sticks for you, First Dog," Daisie spluttered at last. "There aren't any here."

They got up and ran into the sea.

"Ow!" shrieked Becca as Daisie splashed her. "Just you wait, Daisie Trevelyan! I'll get you!"

"Hey!" called Daisie. "Look at those two!"

A woman and a girl, both wearing swimsuits, had come out of one of the new houses. The woman spread a towel over a flat rock. The girl scrambled down to the beach and

15

began wandering about, kicking at the sand. The woman must have turned on a radio; they could make out a faint, tinny sound of music. Then she picked up a magazine.

The girl was acting bored, picking up pebbles and tossing them around. Drac froze to attention – now *that* looked promising. He went bounding up the beach, barking excitedly – Me! Me! Throw one for me!

The girl backed away. Drac joined in her game. Then he followed her down to the water's edge.

"Call your dog off!" the girl yelled, in a high-pitched, bossy sort of voice.

Drac splish-splashed delightedly in and out of the waves, shaking himself wildly.

The girl screamed and leapt back. "I'm soaked!" she complained.

Daisie laughed. "That's what swimsuits are for, my worm." She grabbed Drac's collar. "My dog won't hurt you," she said. "He's not much more than a puppy."

The girl glared at her. "Don't you know this beach is private?"

"No, it isn't," said Daisie. "There aren't any private beaches in Cornwall."

"Well, this one is."

"So where's the notice?" challenged Daisie. "Go on. Show us the notice."

"I will!" The girl strode angrily across the sand. Then she stopped and turned. "There

16

doesn't *have* to be a notice, you know," she said haughtily. She began staring at Daisie. "But I've seen you before," she said. She sounded quite shocked.

Daisie scooped up Drac, squirming and wriggling, and tucked him under one arm. Then she stared right back. "I've seen you, too," she muttered.

The two girls stood, eyeing each other like enemies.

And all the time, Becca felt as if she was watching something on the telly, as if a screen had grown up between herself and the others, cutting them off, turning them into part of some crazy film.

Not real, she thought. *Not true.*

She looked again to check. The girl's hair was tied back, and Daisie's was wild – sticky and salty from the sea. The girl's swimsuit was turquoise, with a pattern of leaves, while Daisie wore a Tregennack Juniors T-shirt over damp cotton shorts.

But the two faces were identical.

CHAPTER THREE

"You're twins," gasped Becca, looking at the matched pair of broad, freckled noses, the same round chins, the same wide mouths, the same greenish-blue eyes fringed with the same gingery lashes.

"Don't talk so daft," muttered Daisie, her eyes still fixed on the girl's face. "How could we be twins?"

The girl stared back at Daisie. "She's nothing like me," she said, turning away. "For one thing, she's common."

"Who are you calling common, my handsome?" yelled Daisie, shocked out of the spell. "I wouldn't want to look like you anyway! You're just a snooty, stuck-up emmet, that's what you are!" She put Drac down on the sand. "Go on, boy! Emmets! Get her!" She paused. "Get her, Drac – u – la!" she said, pronouncing the dog's name very carefully.

The girl backed off nervously. "Who's Dracula?"

"My dog," said Daisie coolly. "He's a vampire. There aren't many vampire dogs, but he's one." As if to prove it, Drac leapt up at the girl, making her skip backwards. "It's a special breed," Daisie added casually. "You only find them in Cornwall."

The girl began screeching. "Get him away! Get him off me!"

Daisie smiled, enjoying herself. "It may already be too late," she murmured. "We can't do a thing if he's tasted your blood."

But Becca'd had enough. "Oh, stop it," she said. "She's scared. Can't you see?"

"I don't like being called common," said Daisie.

"Sorry," mumbled the girl.

"I didn't hear you," said Daisie loudly.

"Sorry! Sorry! Sorry!" The girl was jumping about.

Daisie made a grab for Drac. "And he was only trying to be friendly." She held him out. "Why don't you give him a stroke? That would calm him down."

The girl slumped on to the sand. Her face had gone pink. "I'm not used to dogs," she said.

"You a cat person then?" asked Daisie, but the girl shook her head.

"No cat either?" said Daisie.

"Don't you have any pets?" asked Becca.

"We can't," said the girl. "My mother travels a lot. We move around."

But Daisie couldn't imagine anyone living without animals. "You could have a hamster," she pointed out. "Hamsters are easy."

"I couldn't take it to Switzerland."

"You live in *Switzerland*?" exclaimed Becca.

"Sometimes. Sometimes it's Italy. Venice. Rome. Last year it was California." The girl sighed. "I've always wanted a cat."

"Have one of our kittens, then," offered Daisie.

"She couldn't, dumb-dumb," said Becca. "Don't you see? She could take it out but she'd never get it back in. Rabies, remember?"

Drac wriggled free. He stood for a few moments, contemplating the girl. Suddenly he trotted over and climbed into her lap. The girl stiffened and drew back.

Daisie was furious. "Come here at once!" she shouted. "You bad dog!"

Drac stretched out his chin against the girl's leg.

Daisie gasped. "He never does that with strangers."

The girl gave a nervous smile. "He won't bite?"

Becca grinned. "You believed her vampire story!"

The girl looked annoyed. "Don't be stupid."

She touched the dog's head. "But why call him Dracula?"

"My rotten little brother's into vampire films," explained Daisy. "It was his idea. It's a good name, though. Scares people." She giggled. "Until they see him." Drac yawned, snuffled, then settled down. Daisie reached out. "Shall I take him off you?"

But the girl shook her head. "He's OK," she said.

A woman's voice began calling, "Per-dee-ta! Per-dee-ta! You all right?"

The girl turned and sighed. Then she yelled back, "Yes!"

"That your mum?" asked Daisie.

"My *mum*?" The girl looked offended. "That's Inga. Our au pair. Swedish. Boring. My mother won't be down for another couple of weeks."

"What was that she was calling you?" asked Becca.

"Perdita." The girl laughed. "*Perdeeta!* She can never get it right."

"What's a perdita?" asked Daisie.

"That's my name."

"Never heard of it," said Daisie.

"It was my mother's idea. She'd been to see this play. There was a girl in it called Perdita. It means the Lost One."

"Was she trying to lose you, then?" teased Daisie.

The girl flushed. "I'm very close to my mother."

"Sorry," said Daisie.

"But how did you come out looking just like Daisie?" asked Becca. "Because you do."

"How would I know?" The girl looked at Daisie. "Could you and I be related?"

"But even sisters and cousins don't come out looking the same," argued Becca. "Only twins do that. And even they have to be identical." She turned to Daisie. "Did your mum have twins? Did she lose one?" She giggled. "Maybe that's why *her* mum called her Perdita – because someone had lost her."

"Maybe it was *my* mother who had the twins," remarked Perdita coldly. "Maybe she gave one away to this ancient Cornish-woman…"

"My mum's not old!" said Daisie, furious. "And I even look like her a bit."

"You look more like Perdita," said Becca. "Listen, if you two swapped clothes, I wouldn't know which was which!"

"Doubles," Perdita said slowly. "We're doubles, that's what we are." She stared at Daisie. "Let's try it out."

"How?"

"On her. Dumb Inga. Let's really swap clothes."

Becca could see Daisie was tempted.

"It wouldn't work," she was saying, her

eyes all shiny. "You talk posh, for one thing. She'd never think I was you."

"Makes no difference," said Perdita. "Don't you see? Her English is rotten – she'd never guess."

Daisie made up her mind.

"You're on," she said, scooping the sleeping mongrel out of Perdita's lap and dumping him into Becca's.

Becca sat, watching them padding away over the damp sand, then ducking, giggling, behind a rock. She saw them running into the sea, saw the other girl shaking out her hair and splashing it with water, then finger-combing Daisie's wild mane into a neat bunch.

Drac suddenly jerked upright, aware that Daisie had gone. He wriggled free of Becca's arms and went galloping across the beach, colliding with the girls just as they were coming back.

Daisie and Perdita posed, waiting for Becca to react.

But Becca didn't know what to say or even which of them to speak to. Was it really Daisie in that flash swimsuit? Could that really be posh-voiced Perdita in Daisie's salt-stained shorts?

"Have you really swapped?" she asked weakly. "Or are you having me on?"

The girl in the trendy swimsuit grinned.

"What do you think, my worm?"

"So go on, Daisie," said Perdita. "Dare you! Go up and talk to Inga."

Daisie suddenly looked panicky. "What do I say?"

"Anything." She thought about it. "Tell her you're thirsty. She's got drinks in that cool-box."

"I can't," Daisie wailed.

"Oh, go on, Daisie," urged Becca. "You'll be sorry if you don't."

"But what if she catches on?"

"So what if she does?" said Perdita. "It's not a crime."

"OK, then," said Daisie. "You two hang on to Drac, though. He'd really blow it!"

They watched Daisie reluctantly walking towards the houses. They saw the woman sit up.

"She's got no clothes on!" said Becca, embarrassed.

Perdita yawned. "Thinks she's sexy. Always showing off her boobs. Whips off her top whenever the sun comes out."

Becca could see Daisie moving self-consciously, as if she was acting in the end-of-term show. Then she seemed to relax, squatting on the grass and hugging her knees.

The woman opened a box and took out some cans. Daisie picked one up and waved it in their direction, as if she was saying, "Cheers!"

Becca jumped about. "She's made it! She's made it!"

But Perdita went quiet.

"You know something?" she said at last. "We could do anything, Daisie and me!"

CHAPTER
FOUR

Daisie came running back, hugging three cans.

She collapsed on to the sand, throwing them one each. "She said," she spluttered, taking a slurp of Pepsi and hiccoughing loudly. "She said," she went on when she'd stopped giggling. "She said, what have you done to your hair, Per-dee-ta?" She woke up Drac, rolled him over and began tickling his tummy.

But Perdita wasn't laughing. "We must never be seen together," she said.

"Why not?" Becca was puzzled. "Don't you *want* to show yourselves off? Make everyone think you're twins?"

"I can't wait to show us off to my mum," said Daisie. "She'll never believe it!"

"There are more interesting things we could do first," said Perdita mysteriously.

"Like what?" asked Daisie.

"We could *really* change places," said

26

Perdita. "Fool people." She looked hard at Daisie. "For instance, we're going to St Ives next week. My mother likes me to get culture and stuff, and Inga's into art." She yawned dramatically. "I'm not. Are you?"

"I like looking at pictures," said Daisie. "And I liked going to the new Tate on that school trip."

"Want to go again?" asked Perdita casually.

Becca gasped. "You're nuts," she said. "Daisie could fool Inga for a few minutes but not all day."

But Daisie's eyes were shining. "Want to bet?"

"So what would *you* do?" Becca asked Perdita. "While Daisie was taking your place?" It was only a game, she thought. A pretend. A what-if?

"Someone would have to take Daisie's place."

Daisie burst out laughing. "At Mum's?" She shook her head. "You'd never fool my mum."

"Listen. You tell your mum you're going out." Perdita pointed at Becca. "Seeing *her*, if you like."

Becca suddenly found herself cut off, almost eavesdropping on their plans.

"Then you come here," Perdita went on. "And we swap clothes on the beach. You stay, and I turn up as you. Simple."

Becca tried to join in. "I could even walk over with *Daisie*," she offered, "and then walk back

27

with *you*." Brilliant, she thought, pleased with herself.

"No." It was Perdita's game and she was running it. "You'd know who I really was. You wouldn't be able to act natural with Daisie's mother. You'd give the game away."

"No, I wouldn't," said Becca, hurt.

But Daisie was looking as if she'd just won the raffle at the school fête. "Let's do it!" she yelled.

Perdita shook her head. "Let's go and change back into our own things," she said. "Then we can talk about it."

Silly old Daisie, thought Becca, watching them go. She takes everything so seriously...

On the way home, they quarrelled again.

"It was a daft idea anyway," argued Becca.

"We know that," said Daisie airily. "We're not ready yet, are we? We've got to work up to it slowly, Dita says. She's coming to my place tomorrow."

"She's only an emmet," Becca pointed out. "Only a summer visitor. How's she going to find it?"

"They've got a street map, stupid. And she'll get Inga to drive her over and drop her off at the top of my street." She looked smug. "I'm meeting her there at eleven."

"The two of you'll be seen when you walk back."

28

"No, we won't." Daisie smiled. "Dita says people don't look much at your face when you're just walking past. And Mum's seeing patients then, so she won't be around, and Ben'll be out playing football. We'll just change clothes and try it out, like she said. See what happens. Then I'll go out, and Dita'll take over until dinner-time."

"Dita, Dita," repeated Becca scornfully. "It's almost as stupid as Perdita. Anyway, it won't work. Can you imagine that girl coping with your kittens, your guinea-pigs, your terrapins and your brother's worm farm? Not to mention Drac."

"She was OK with Drac," said Daisie, "once she stopped being scared."

"And your mum would never believe in that twitty posh voice…"

"You don't like Perdita," said Daisie. "Do you?"

"Not much," growled Becca. "No."

The next morning it rained, silently, in fine, silvery-white veils that drifted inland from the sea.

Becca came down late. Dad had long since left, and so had their summer visitors, packing wellies and oilskins for their trek across the moor.

Mum had made them a hot breakfast and a packed lunch. The kitchen still smelt of fry-up.

29

Becca poured out some tea from the pot. "You know that girl?" she said.

"What girl?"

"The one I told you about last night," said Becca irritably. "The one who looks just like Daisie Trevelyan."

"Don't forget your vitamin pill," said Mum, plonking one down beside Becca's cornflakes. "You don't want to be sniffling when you start your new school."

"I'm not sniffling now." Becca gulped back the pill. "She's Daisie's *double*, Mum," she said. "Honest."

But Mum had switched on the Hoover. "Daisie's what?" she yelled.

"Double!" yelled Becca.

Mum smiled at her vaguely. "Oh, yes, lovely," she said.

Becca gave up. She washed her plate and her mug. Then she pottered around, half-watching a cartoon on the telly, and playing with Cleo, her long-haired grey cat.

The front door bell rang. Mum switched off the Hoover. "New coat?" Becca heard her exclaim.

Then Daisie came swanking into the back room, whirling around, showing herself off.

"What d'you think? What d'you think?"

She took off the yellow showerproof with the scarlet and blue lining and threw it at Becca. "Catch! Try it on! And look at these!"

she added, dancing around in scarlet and blue leggings and a blue sweatshirt. "Her mum works in these fashion shops! BREAKTHROUGH, they're called."

"I like this," said Becca, smoothing down the coat.

"Whose mum works in which fashion shops?" asked Mum.

Daisie put a finger against her lips. "Just someone my mum knows," she said, looking at Becca. "So she can get these things cheap."

"Useful," Mum murmured, switching the Hoover back on.

"Don't tell her," mouthed Daisie. "Please don't tell her," she repeated as they walked upstairs. "Not yet, anyway. It would ruin everything."

"OK," promised Becca. Then she thought of something. "So what's that girl wearing?"

"Dita?" Daisie giggled. "My old jeans and a Save the Whales T-shirt!"

CHAPTER
FIVE

Becca tried not to be jealous but she just couldn't help it. Why did all the interesting things happen to Daisie?

She began studying her own face in the bathroom mirror. She ruffled her fringe and stared deeply into her own conker-brown eyes. Did *she* have a double? she wondered. Did everyone?

"Does everyone have a double?" she asked Dad at supper.

"What a daft question," said Dad. "No one has a double. Except identical twins."

Daisie topped up the water in Drac's bowl.

"Can people have doubles?" she asked Mum.

Mum thought about it. "I've read somewhere," she said at last, "that we all have doubles. Though I really don't know."

"Maybe face designs run out," said Daisie. "And then they have to repeat themselves."

"Maybe," agreed Mum. She paused. "Daisie, did you *have* to put on that silly voice again this morning?"

"You mean, this voice?" And Daisie mimicked Perdita's high-pitched tones.

Mum sighed. "I think we've had enough of that one, don't you?"

"You say the same thing about my Cornish," grumbled Daisie. "Then when I speak posh, you go on about that."

Daisie began to be obsessed by clothes shops.

When she and Becca rode into Penzance on the bus, they didn't spend much time browsing for bargains any more, or hanging around the quay, watching the boats unload.

Becca was bored. "Let's *do* something," she complained.

"If you like." Daisie sighed. "Penzance clothes shops are a dead loss anyway. They don't have a thing that's as brilliant as Dita's."

Going down to the beach wasn't the same, either.

They didn't climb over to the cove because they just felt like going. It was all arranged. Perdita would have rung Daisie or Daisie would have rung Perdita. Then Daisie'd ask Becca as an afterthought.

But Daisie and Dita didn't *need* anyone else.

They were like two mirrors, reflecting only each other.

"I wonder how I'd look in one of those plaits," Daisie'd say, weaving one into Dita's hair.

"You should try jeans cut like this." And Dita would pose like a sexy fashion model. "From one of my mother's new shops. I'll give you a pair." Then she'd nudge Daisie. "They'd look just as good on you." And the two of them would laugh.

They weren't really like twins, decided Becca. Twins were two separate people. This was like having your own reflection as a best friend.

But although she was just a hanger-on, she kept going out with them. The holidays would be over in a few weeks, she thought. That girl's mother would turn up and the three of them would go back to wherever they came from. Switzerland. America. Becca didn't care.

They were only emmets, even if they *were* rich…

Then the girls began playing tricks on Becca.

One morning, she met Perdita in the post office.

"Hi!" said Becca awkwardly, gaping at the rainbow sweatshirt and the stripy leggings.

Perdita'd looked at her distantly. "Oh, hullo, Becca," she'd said. "I'm sending these cards to my mother." Her voice sounded stilted, strange.

But when Becca followed her out, "Perdita" turned and poked her. "Caught you, my worm," teased Daisie. "Didn't I? Didn't I?"

And then there was the day Perdita came to tea.

Becca'd asked Daisie.

It was raining that day; solid sheets of rain that kept even the summer visitors in, watching old films.

"Good weather for ducks," said Mr Graham, settling down.

"Hope it clears up tomorrow," said Mrs Graham anxiously. "We've only got three days left."

"That's Cornwall for you," said Mr Graham.

Becca'd pottered around, bored. Then she'd rung Daisie. "Want to come over?" she'd asked. "Stay and have tea. Mum'll get something good – the emmets had to stay in."

At half past three, she'd seen Daisie running up the path, a sodden Drac at her heels and rain bouncing off the hood of her oilskin.

"Hi!" called Becca.

"You're a wet one," said Mum.

They towelled Drac dry, then went upstairs.

"What shall we do?" asked Daisie.

Becca brought out some cards. "Racing Canfield?"

Daisie looked baffled. "Whatever's that?"

"Daisie?" Becca flicked her fingers into Daisie's face. "*Racing Canfield*," she repeated. "We *always* play it! Remember?"

Daisie started fiddling with a hole in her jumper.

"Daisie?" Becca repeated. Then she caught on. "Perdita! You pig!"

Perdita looked smug. "Fooled you, though, didn't I? Fooled your mother too."

"But the clothes? How did you do it?"

"Easy." Perdita ruffled Drac's fur. "I arranged it with Daisie."

Becca's head was spinning. "So where's Daisie now?"

"Back home."

"And Inga?"

"Oh, Inga dropped me by the church an hour ago. I told her I didn't like being ferried from house to house like some infant. She's picking me up at six." Dita grinned. "So I could stay to tea."

"You weren't invited," said Becca.

"Who cares, my bird?" It sounded ridiculous when Perdita said it.

They played awkward games, filling in time.

"What's your mother actually do?" asked Becca.

Dita sighed. "I've told you already."

"I know it's clothes," said Becca awkwardly. "But you don't get that rich working in clothes

36

shops." She straightaway wished she hadn't said that – it sounded so rude.

But Perdita wasn't bothered. "Depends on the shops," she said airily, "and whether you own them."

Becca quickly changed the subject. "What about your dad?"

Perdita stiffened. "He was a failure," she said briefly. "And my mother doesn't go for failures."

Becca winced. Dita sounded like Dad going through one of her school reports – Fair... Rebecca is capable of better work... Should try harder...

"He must have felt a bit funny," she said, "when your mum was so clever."

Perdita shrugged. "Who cares? He's not around any more, is he? Same as Daisie's dad."

"It's *not* the same as Daisie's dad," said Becca fiercely. "Daisie's dad's away looking for work. That's why he isn't around much."

"Same thing," observed Perdita. "And all that aromatherapy stuff Daisie's mum does – she's the one who makes the loot."

Tea had been a nightmare, with the girls not really speaking, and Perdita saying "please" and "thank you" and "Could you pass the biscuits, Mrs Hughes?" to Becca's mum.

"What a very well-bred child that was,"

said Mrs Graham approvingly, after Perdita had left.

But Mum was giving Becca a very funny look.

"Is your friend Daisie sickening for something?" she said at last. "Because that's not the Daisie I used to know…"

CHAPTER
SIX

Daisie's house smelt of onions and dog. It smelt of drying herbs and breakfast toast and cat-food and seaweed. There were dribbles of milk across the grey stone floor, and odd socks steaming in front of the stove.

Daisie's mum strode into the kitchen, her big, freckled hands still scented with massage oil.

Perdita checked on the time, concealing her Rolex. "Don't you have another patient – " it was so hard to say it – "Mum?"

"Want to get rid of me?" said Daisie's mum, plugging in the kettle.

"Oh no, of course not," said Perdita quickly.

Daisie's mum shook her head. "You're in a funny state these days, Daisie Trevelyan."

Perdita bent over the kitten asleep on her knees. "What do you mean?" she mumbled.

"That silly posh voice you keep putting on,

for one thing." Daisie's mum sighed. "It's stopped being funny. If it ever was."

"Sorry," whispered Dita.

"And have you been borrowing someone's clothes? Ben said he saw you in the park the other day, all dressed up like a dog's dinner."

Perdita changed the subject by sneezing loudly.

"And you're getting a cold," said Daisie's mum. "Vitamins for you, my girl. And a good going over with oil of lavender." The doorbell rang, and she gulped back her tea. "Here I go again," she said. "Work, work, work."

But halfway along the passage, she stopped and turned. "Fix Charles and Di," she yelled. "And the guinea-pigs. And make up a bowl for the vampire, or he'll be starting on us!"

Ten minutes later, when Daisie let herself in, she found Perdita struggling with a large can of dog food.

"Don't give him all that," Daisie whispered, horrified. She took the can out of Perdita's hands and spooned back some of the food. "And he gets kitchen scraps, too. And a mixer."

"What's a mixer?" whispered Perdita.

Daisie hauled out a big bag of things that looked like crusts. "This," she said. (She would have added "dumb-dumb" if it hadn't been Dita.) She dumped two handfuls on top of the dog food. Then she chopped up some greens and put those in too.

Dita wrinkled her nose. "That looks revolting!" She pointed. "Did you know you've got a snail on your ceiling?"

"Oh, that's the Martian," said Daisie. "He belongs to Mum."

Confused, Dita wandered over to the terrapin tank. "And how do you fix these two?"

"Charles and Di? Oh, they get cat food…" Daisie suddenly grabbed her. "Look out, there's Ben!" she said. "Quick!"

The two girls belted upstairs. They could hear Ben crashing around, calling, "Hey, Daisie?"

"He sometimes barges in," whispered Daisie, bolting the door.

"Who've you got up there?"

"No one," yelled Daisie. "I'll be down in a sec!"

The two girls quickly changed clothes. Perdita sneezed.

"If you've got a cold," whispered Daisie, "you'd better get rid of it. Or give it to me."

"Why should I give it to you?"

Daisie sighed. Dita might be rich, she thought, but she wasn't very bright. "Because we can't have just *one* of us with a cold," she said. "Can we?"

"Oh," whispered Perdita. "I hadn't thought of that."

* * *

41

Dita let herself out while Daisie distracted Ben.

At the top of the street, Inga was waiting for her in the car. She was looking cross.

"That little man," she complained, starting the engine. "He think he is gift of God to women."

"What man?" asked Perdita.

"Mr Sparrow," said Inga. "You know – that man from the estate office."

Dita giggled. "You mean, Tweetie Pie? What's he doing around here?"

Inga sighed. "He drive past. Then he see me. He stop, park, come over. How is everything? he ask me *again*. If there is anything more we can do … *you* know."

They turned on to the main road out of Tregennack.

"Maybe he fancies you," teased Perdita.

"I have boyfriend already," said Inga virtuously. "In Stockholm."

They parked next to a BMW. "New people," explained Inga. "They move in this morning. While you were out with your new friend." She smiled. "We go on expedition this afternoon, Perdeeta, yes?"

That evening, Dita's mother rang.

"Hi, Liz," said Dita, taking the phone from Inga.

"How's my best girl?"

"I'm OK."

"What did you do today?"

"Inga took me to a lighthouse."

"Sounds like fun." Dita heard the usual breathy pause that meant Liz was smoking. "Inga tells me you've made some nice new friends down there…"

"Oh, yes!" said Perdita. "And they've got a dog called Dracula, and terrapins in a tank and guinea-pigs and worms and a snail who's a Martian." She giggled. "They're crazy! And they've got cats, too, and one of the cats has got kittens and I'm having one."

"Calm down," said Perdita's mother. "And be sensible. You know we can't."

"Oh, but wait till you see it," said Dita. She hesitated. "Liz, do you think people can have doubles?"

Her mother laughed. "Only twins."

"Liz, did *you* have twins?" asked Perdita. "I mean, was I meant to be part of two?"

"Dita?" said her mother. "What kinds of videos have you been watching?"

"Nothing," said Perdita. "I was just wondering, that's all. And Liz?"

"Yes?"

"When are you coming down?"

There was a long silence.

"Liz?"

"We've had a few setbacks, sweetie." Dita heard the click of a lighter. "Some idiot broke into the London flat…"

43

Dita gasped. "That's awful! What did he take?"

"Nothing much," said her mother brightly. "Nothing of yours, love. A nice, clean burglary, the police called it, but I'll have to fly back in a day or two to sort things out. We'll have to check on our security. Thank goodness you and I were both away."

Dita shivered. "Supposing we hadn't been..."

"Well, we were, so don't worry. It came at a bad time, though." Liz gave a tight little laugh. "I'm facing some tough opposition over these new Swiss shops. I think we'll have it all stitched up by next week, in spite of everything – we don't call ourselves the BREAKTHROUGH chain for nothing, do we?"

"We're the greatest," said Dita loyally.

"So I'd give it about ten days. Maybe a bit longer. Then we'll have fun together. Won't we?"

Ten more days, thought Perdita.

Just ten more days of sometimes being Daisie...

CHAPTER SEVEN

Next morning, Becca and Daisie went over to the cove. "Dita's got a cold," explained Daisie. "So we can't do proper swaps."

Perdita sat waiting for them, listening to her Walkman. The minute Drac spotted her, he began whimpering with pleasure. Then he jumped on her back, making her scream.

"Drac!" bellowed Daisie. "Come here at once!" She was beginning to feel cross. Drac was *her* dog, not Dita's.

It had been the same with the kittens. Dita'd just chosen one. "This one's mine," she'd said.

Later, Daisie, Ben and Mum had been thinking up names. "He's Ninja," said Ben, "'cause he's a fighter. And that one's Supercat."

"Well, this one's Christopher Columbus," giggled Daisie. "Because he's an explorer."

"That's funny," said Mum. "You called him Tom this morning." And Daisie had felt cheated. What right had Dita to name one of their kittens? She'd said she couldn't have one. So what business was it of hers?

Dita switched off the Walkman and blew her nose loudly. "I'm taking lots of vitamins," she said. "And we've been looking everywhere for oil of lavender."

But that was *Mum's* way of curing a cold, thought Daisie. So did this girl have part shares in Mum as well?

"Look at that lot..." Becca pointed at people setting up a picnic on the beach. "It isn't our desert island any more."

"And that's only the beginning..." Perdita groaned. "Wait till the rest of those houses get filled. Old Tweetie Pie'll be rubbing his hands. He kept saying we wouldn't be lonely. Ugh!"

"Who's Tweetie Pie?" asked Becca.

"The guy from the estate office. Mr Sparrow." Perdita pulled a face. "Smarmy," she said. "He turned up the day after we arrived. To settle us in – as if we needed him. He's a creep. Insisted on taking a photo of us for their books. Their first clients, he told us. Smarm, smarm. But I know why he really did it. Guess what?" She grinned. "He fancies Inga!"

Daisie was looking thoughtful. "I suppose those houses are really posh inside..."

Dita got up. "Why don't you come and look?"

The three of them walked up the beach past the picnic party. Inga was lying on her tummy, toasting her back. She opened her eyes briefly. "Your friends stay for lunch?"

The girls looked at each other questioningly, but Dita shook her head. "Not yet," she whispered. "No, they can't," she said aloud.

They clutched at each other, giggling, as they walked up to the house. What would Inga have said if she'd seen two Perditas?

"*Tweens!*" announced Dita, making fun of Inga's accent.

"*Tweens! Tweens! Ja-ja!*" repeated the others, fooling around.

The valley where the houses stood was speckled with flowers – moon daisies and yarrow and sea lavender – but the gardens and terraces were small and neat, paved with pale new stone and set with picnic tables and parasols and palm trees in pots.

Perdita unlocked the front door and they followed her in. They walked through a lobby with coats and boots, and then into a hall with little pink wall lamps and a large, gold-framed mirror that reflected a stiff arrangement of gladioli and lilies in a shiny brass pot.

"What's this for?" asked Becca, touching a small, glass-fronted box.

"Don't set that off!" Perdita tugged her away. "It's our alarm system."

"*Alarm system?*" Daisie laughed. "Dita,

this is Cornwall, not London."

They walked into a room with flowered chintz sofas and a polished wood floor. Drac made for the kitchen, skidding on a rug, and they followed him in, making little trails of sand across the black and white tiles.

"Oh, it's so glittery," sighed Daisie. "It's so grand." She wriggled on to one of the bar stools and curled her toes around its legs. "Bring me a drink, waiter," she ordered.

"At once, madam." Perdita opened the fridge. "Pepsi? Crush? Fruit juice?"

"Gin and tonic," joked Daisie.

Dita snapped open a Pepsi and stood it in front of her. "I'm afraid we're out of gin, madam."

"Never mind." Daisie stroked her hair, brushed back like Perdita's now, and caught in a plait. "And find us a bowl, my worm, do," she added. "There's a thirsty dog down there." She stuck a straw into the can and sat, swinging her legs and listening to Drac slurping up the water. "I like this place," she said dreamily. Then she remembered something. "Isn't it my turn to come here? We always do swaps in my place or Becca's."

"I'd better show you around first," said Perdita. "Or Inga might think something funny was going on."

"Mum didn't," Daisie pointed out.

That's what you think, thought Dita. She

48

led them back into the main room. "That's for the telly and this is for the video." She showed Daisie the controls. "There's a camcorder somewhere, too, if you want to use it…"

"Wouldn't know how, my bird," said Daisie.

They went upstairs.

"Inga's room," announced Perdita. They caught a glimpse of magazines scattered across a lacy coverlet. "And this one will be Liz's room, if she ever turns up."

"Is Liz your sister?" asked Becca.

"Liz is my mother."

"Your *mother*?"

Perdita laughed. "Liz can't stand being called Mum." She opened more doors. "Loo… Bathroom…"

"What's that thing?" asked Daisie.

"It's a *Jacuzzi*. Makes bubbles. Watch." Dita turned on the tap and the water swirled and frothed.

"Wow!" said Daisie. "I can't wait."

"Neither can Drac!" screeched Becca, making a grab.

"Oh, no!" Daisie wailed. "But he *hates* baths."

"He thinks it's the sea," giggled Dita. "That's different."

Daisie hauled Drac out and rolled him up in a towel. "So let's see your room."

"It's nothing special," said Dita, pushing

open a door. "Oh, the cleaning woman's been messing things up again," she complained, shifting a half-bald teddy from a shelf to the bed.

Becca looked at the mirrored wardrobes and the flower-printed curtains with their matching blinds. She looked at the pine chest of drawers with its gold-tasselled lamp, and the framed prints of sailing ships on the blue-and-white striped wallpaper. It was like walking into a picture from a magazine.

"Bring any card games?" she asked, sitting on the bed.

"No point. No one to play them with."

"Any books then?"

Perdita sighed. "You sound a bit like my mother." She yawned. "As far as I'm concerned, books are for school. I've got a Gameboy, though. And one of these." She took a disc out of its case and slipped it into a portable CD player. "Do you go for Rap?" she asked them, capering about.

But Daisie was already riffling through Dita's wardrobe. "I want to try on this," she was saying. "Oh, and this." She slipped on a swirly summer dress.

Perdita grinned. "I didn't realize I looked so good in that."

"You look amazing in it!" sang Daisie.

They were doing it again, thought Becca.

"You're my reflection," said Dita.

"No, I'm not," said Daisie. "Put this on. See? Now you're mine."

Becca was feeling left out again. She began pottering about, picking things up, pretending not to care.

"What's his name?" she asked, fiddling with the bear. Then she picked up a photograph. "And who's the guy with the eyebrows?"

"None of your business!" Dita's face was suddenly flushed and angry. She lunged at Becca, snatching back the photograph. "And leave my things alone!" she yelled.

Becca was shocked. "Sorry," she said, furious with herself for saying something so stupid. She noticed Drac trying to wriggle free of his bath towel. "Shall I take him outside?" she offered quickly. "He's a bit fed up."

"How do you know he's fed up?" challenged Daisie. "He's not your dog, is he?"

But Drac struggled to the floor and followed Becca out.

She turned and ruffled his still-damp fur. "Good old Drac," she said. "You've had enough of them, boy, haven't you? And so've I."

She ran past the palm trees and climbed down to the rocks. Then she picked up a pebble.

"Fetch it, vampire!" she yelled.

CHAPTER EIGHT

Daisie rang next morning.

"I've got a spot," she wailed.

"So what?" said Becca. "You won't die."

"And Dita's got the flu or something."

"She'll be OK," said Becca, hoping she wouldn't.

"But you don't understand," said Daisie. "We were going for the big one on Thursday."

"The big what?"

"The big swap, dumb-dumb. All day. Me to St Ives and her to Mum's."

"It wouldn't have worked," said Becca. "They'd guess. Ben would guess. She couldn't keep it up all day. And neither could you."

Perdita lay on the sofa, watching TV.

"I want another drink," she croaked. "And some more vitamins."

"No more pills," said Inga. "You have

"enough swallowed."

"What do you know?" grumbled Dita. She wished she could talk to Daisie's mum. Daisie's mum would have fixed her cold.

Bored, she switched channels. Sunlight was bleaching out the colours, making everything look washy.

She put a hand on her forehead. Was she running a temperature? Was it a cold or was it flu?

They simply *had* to do it on Thursday, she thought. That show was on for only three days. The Topsy-Turvey Theatre Company and Martin's name on the posters – what incredible luck! She could hardly believe it.

She could get Inga to take her, cancel the trip to St Ives, but she'd be taking a risk. Inga'd almost certainly blab to Liz.

And if it was just a cold, she thought, it wouldn't really matter. She grinned. Daisie's mum might even give her that lavender oil massage.

And Inga'd never notice Daisie's spot.

It would be the most brilliant thing to do. He'd be so impressed when she told him.

She'd always known he'd be famous.

If it *was* him...

She went up to the bathroom and checked on her face. It was awful. Her nose was dripping, and the skin round her eyes was pink and puffy. Too much English weather, Inga'd said, making one of her feeble jokes.

But now it was sunny, and sun was good for colds. She might even go outside, Dita thought, and lie on the beach.

She just *had* to get better by Thursday.

What would *he* think if he saw her looking like that?

A new spot was flourishing next to the first one.

Daisie squeezed it, then dabbed it with marigold cream. "Go away, you horrible thing," she muttered. "You'll spoil everything."

It had all gone so brilliantly up to now. There was even that show. That had been Dita's idea. It would use up most of the afternoon, she'd said. Get her out of the house.

Oh, that girl was brilliant, thought Daisie admiringly.

Ben gawped at Daisie's face when she went downstairs. "You've got another one," he told her. "And the first one's just going to pop!"

"Oh, shut up, Ben," said Daisie, "or I'll hit you!" She turned to Mum. "Can I go to that show on Thursday? The one in Barnicoat's Fields? I've got enough pocket money."

"Why not?" said Mum. "Take Ben along too."

Daisie had to think quickly. Dita'd never be able to cope with Ben. "I'm actually going with Becca," she fibbed. "Becca's already got the tickets."

"We could always stretch to another one."

"Oh, Mum," grumbled Daisie. "We planned to go *together*."

"Mean old things," said Ben.

Mum ruffled his hair. "Never you mind, my handsome," she said. "You can come with me. I'll buy us chocolates. We'll go together on Saturday afternoon."

Becca, too, had seen the posters.

"There's a show on," she told Mum. "Over in Barnicoat's Fields. Something called the Topsy-Turvey Theatre Company."

"What a silly name," said Mum. "Anyway, aren't you a bit old for that sort of thing?"

"Wasn't going," said Becca. "It's all this stuff about King Arthur." She pulled a face. "They only put it on for the emmets."

Mum looked annoyed. "I've told you before," she said. "Don't call summer visitors that."

"Why not?" said Becca. "Everyone else does."

"Then maybe we're the only ones with good manners," snapped Mum.

But Becca was sick of good manners. Good manners stopped you saying what you knew was true. Summer visitors *were* emmets. They stuffed themselves with pasties and clotted cream, and trundled caravans down narrow lanes, and ruined wild, secret places with stupid developments like Smugglers Cove.

That girl Dita was a right emmet. With that silly name and all those fancy clothes, what did she know about anything real?

Daisie'd been real, thought Becca sadly. But now she was like someone under a spell. *Her* spell.

Spots, for instance. The old Daisie wouldn't have noticed. The old Daisie wouldn't have fussed about clothes, either.

Becca longed for September, when the visitors would be gone, when the two spare rooms would be spare again and Mum would have time to listen.

Then she and Daisie would slowly wake up, as if from some awful summer dream.

For nobody could have a double.

Only twins…

CHAPTER NINE

Daisie came running up the path with Drac at her heels.

"Here comes your well-bred friend again," teased Becca's mum. "Just as well the Grahams didn't hear *my bird, my worm*."

"What's wrong with things like that?" asked Becca. "If that's the way she wants to speak, then it's OK." She opened the front door. "Hi, Daisie." She hesitated. "It *is* Daisie, isn't it?"

"Listen." Daisie breathed at her. "No sniffles," she said. "Coming for a walk?"

"Where to?" asked Becca warily.

"Oh, not Smugglers Cove," said Daisie. "Dita's staying in."

"I'm going out with Daisie!" Becca yelled happily. It was just like the old days, as if Dita had never happened.

"Don't be late for lunch, then," said Mum, "or you won't get any!"

The two girls walked down the lane, then scrambled over a stile. Daisie was hatching something. Becca could tell.

They walked past the old tin mine.

Drac saw a rabbit.

"Come out of there!" shrieked Daisie. "This minute! At once!"

They sprawled on the soft hill grass. Drac nosed at the air, still picking up rabbit scent. Then he gave up, defeated, and settled down.

"Guess what?" said Daisie. "I met Tweetie Pie."

"The bloke who fancies Inga?"

Daisie nodded.

"But you don't know him."

Daisie giggled. "I do now." She threw a chewed ball for Drac. "You see, Tweetie Pie met *me*. He thought I was Dita. I was wearing her jacket – you know, the one with the mirror stuff and beads."

"Oh, no!" gasped Becca. "So what happened?"

"He took me for an ice-cream," Daisie crowed. "In that flash new place. One of those Cornish Cream Specials with a Flake and strawberries."

Becca sighed. "Oh, yummy…"

"He wanted to know about Inga, how much time she spent with me – things like that."

"So what did you tell him?"

Daisie laughed. "I made it all up!"

"That's not fair," said Becca, but she was laughing, too. "Have you told Dita?"

"Haven't had time, my worm. But it proves something, doesn't it?"

"What?"

"That me and Dita can fool anyone."

Becca thought of something. "What about her posh voice?"

"I can speak posh, Rebecca Hughes," said Daisie haughtily. Then she laughed. "If I don't have to keep it up too long." She stretched out on the grass. "So Thursday's in the bag."

"What about her cold?" asked Becca. She looked. "What about your spots?"

"They're nearly gone, see? And Dita's better, too."

Pity, thought Becca. She'd imagined Dita getting sicker and sicker, so that she'd have to be whisked back to London. Or Switzerland. Or Venice. Or Timbuctoo.

"Come on," said Daisie.

They climbed up past the monument and on to the coast path. Then they slid down to a rock ledge and sat watching the sea.

"Look, there they are!" said Becca, pointing at the seals.

"M-m-m," said Daisie vaguely. "Listen. You're in the plot too, you know."

"What plot?"

"Thursday, stupid. You've got to do two things."

"So what if I won't?"

"Oh, Becca," groaned Daisie. "It's only for fun. We're coming clean at the weekend. Telling everyone." She grinned. "Can you imagine Mum's face?"

Becca shrugged. "So what do you want me to do?"

"For starters, get two tickets for that Topsy-Turvey show."

"So who's paying?" asked Becca.

Daisie took a fiver out of her pocket and waved it in the air. "She is. She's loaded."

"So who's going?"

"You are," said Daisie. "With Dita."

Becca was horrified. "Oh, no," she said. "Not with her. I won't."

"And we're swapping clothes at your place," went on Daisie, ignoring her. "It makes more sense that way."

"What about Mum?" said Becca. "If Mum saw two Daisie Trevelyans, she'd flip!"

"That's up to you, my handsome."

"Oh, stop putting on the Cornish," said Becca irritably. "No one else round here does."

"That's because they're not me," said Daisie. "That's why."

Thursday dawned, clear, blue and sparkly.

A perfect day, thought Dita as she got into the car.

"I've just got to drop something off at my

friend's house," she said.

Inga looked at her sharply. "Something funny going on."

"What makes you think that?" asked Dita innocently.

Inga shrugged. "This friend. Is a boy?"

"No!" protested Dita.

"OK, OK." Inga parked the car at the top of the lane. "I wait here fifteen minutes," she said, tapping her watch. "Then I come and fetch."

"You wouldn't," shrieked Dita.

"Your mother not like this behaviour," said Inga.

"I'm only seeing my *friend*," insisted Dita. "*She's* called Becca. Rebecca Hughes. You've met her already. On the beach."

"I meet none of your friends," accused Inga. "You all run too fast."

"Well, there aren't any boys," said Dita. "So there."

Daisie and Becca had been looking out for Dita, spying on the road from the room upstairs.

As soon as they saw her, Becca ran down.

"Who's that?" called out Mum.

"Only Daisie," yelled Becca. "She went into the garden and got locked out."

They belted up the stairs and into the bedroom.

Dita grabbed Daisie. "Quick, change!" she

61

urged. "Inga knows something's up!"

"Then we can't do it," said Daisie. "Can we?"

Dita wriggled out of her sandwashed jeans. "Put these on," she said. "Go on. Do it. You can't back out now."

Daisie whipped off her T-shirt and threw it at Dita. Then she pulled on Dita's black and white Lycra sun-top and pranced about, admiring herself. "Mirror, mirror," she chanted. "Do I look good?"

"Who cares?" said Dita. "You've only got five minutes. Inga's in the Fiat. At the top of the lane."

"And watch out for Mum," warned Becca.

Daisie crept out. Then she turned and waved her hands.

St Ives! she thought joyfully. *Here I come!*

CHAPTER TEN

Dita pulled on Daisie's Tregennack Juniors T-shirt. "Walk up with me," she said to Becca. She felt suddenly unsure of herself. How long was the "posh voice" thing going to cover her? Daisie's mum knew there was something wrong.

But it sounded so silly when she tried to say things like "my worm", and she couldn't copy Daisie's accent.

You need an ear for music to do accents, her dad had once said. Well, that counted Dita out. She couldn't sing for toffee.

Anyway, she was mostly Liz's girl, *she* knew that. All set to be a powerful woman like her mother. "We're going to conquer the world," Liz was fond of saying.

But that meant making enemies.

And it meant having your flat broken into because you were hardly ever there...

Becca left her at the top of Daisie's street. "You're on your own now," she said. She sounded almost pleased. "I'll come back for you around three. OK?"

Someone greeted Dita. "Hi, Daisie!"

Dita began hurrying. "Oh, hi!" she called back.

She let herself in with Daisie's key. Drac started to bark. Then he wagged his tail.

There was a basket of crab-apples on the kitchen table, and a big brown pot simmering on top of the stove. Dita plucked Tom out of a sock nest and let him climb about on her shoulders. "You're mine," she told him, but she knew it was a lie.

In a few weeks' time she'd be back in London. And then she'd be starting yet another new school.

Oh, why couldn't she stay in Cornwall for ever? Send Daisie back to London. Daisie'd go for that.

It wasn't that she didn't love Liz, she thought. How many people had a mother like hers? How many other girls had done the things she'd done?

I'll never keep up with you two, Dad had said before he left. Life should be slower, sweeter.

She was supposed to see him sometimes but it never seemed to happen. There were just those chocolates that always arrived late for her birthday.

And those books.

Every Christmas...

Dita heard Daisie's mum seeing a patient out. "'Bye, Mrs Thomas. Take care, now."

Then Ben came crashing in through the back door, his knees splotched with mud. "Hi, spotty," he yelled.

"But they've gone!" Daisie's mum had come breezing into the kitchen in a wave of cinnamon oil. "Look," she said, cupping her hand around Dita's chin. "Not a spot on her. You're a great advertisement, my girl, for that marigold cream." She strode across to the stove, lifted the lid of the pot and sipped at a spoonful of bean stew. "Right," she said, pushing back a strand of her long gingery hair. "Forks and bowls." She clapped her hands. "Get moving!"

Dita looked around wildly, then spotted four gold lustre bowls on the dresser shelf.

Ben gaped and pointed. "Not Grannie's bowls!"

"Maybe it goes along with that new posh voice of hers." Daisie's mum sighed loudly. "Put them back, Daisie, do. You know better than that." She took three blue-and-white bowls from the draining rack and set them out on the table. "Enough nonsense, now," she said, ladling out the stew.

Ben began staring at Dita's watch. "Wow!"

he said. "Where did you get that?"

Dita thought quickly. "Becca lent it to me," she lied. "We swapped. She's got mine."

"Looks a bit expensive," said Daisie's mum. "Better not lose it."

"I'll be careful," said Dita, concentrating on the stew.

Daisie's mum noticed her silence.

"You got the hump, Daisie Trevelyan?"

"Just a headache," muttered Dita.

"Oh!" Daisie's mum was over in a trice, putting her arms round Dita's shoulders. "I thought there was something wrong." She drew back. "You smell different," she said. "You feel different." She frowned, trying to work it out. "I think you must be sickening for something."

Promptly at three, Becca turned up.

"Daisie's in a mood," declared Ben. "Can I have her ticket?"

"I'm OK now," said Dita quickly.

Daisie's mum popped her head round the door of the treatment room. "See you later, lovey," she said. "Clowns'll cheer you up."

They'd set up a table near the entrance to Barnicoat's Fields.

"We don't need to queue," Becca pointed out. "We've got tickets, haven't we?"

"I've got to buy a programme," insisted Dita.

Oh, you're such a fusspot, Becca thought. *Where do you think you are? This isn't posh theatre, like you get up in London. It's only a bunch of hippies dressed up in daft clothes.*

And the queue was full of little kids pushing and shoving, and dripping ice lolly juice down the back of Becca's neck.

Becca had had enough. "I'll go and find us some seats," she said.

She edged between benches, wriggled around knees and nearly knocked over someone's bottle of juice. There was a space at the back, where it would be easy to sneak out if the whole thing got too boring. Becca settled down, folding up her cardigan to keep Dita's place.

The field smelt of hot grass and sweets and popcorn. Behind the enclosure, they'd put up a flimsy painted castle with banners, and a battle tent with flags, and a big round table with armchairs draped in fabric. A wasp zigzagged round her head and she ducked irritably. There was a good film on at the Odeon. If Dita was paying, why not for something like that?

But when the show began, when ladies in tall, floaty headdresses came sweeping across the grass, when the foolish knight on his hobby-horse always got things wrong, when King Arthur held hands with Guinevere, and Merlin arrived in a puff of green smoke, she found she was enjoying it after all.

She turned to say something to Dita, but Dita still wasn't there. She looked around. Could that be her in the front row with all those little kids? Becca picked up her cardigan. That girl was a pain...

The show ended with a flight of silver balloons. Then the knights and the ladies took hands and King Arthur said, "I command all you good people to dance with us at our court."

Becca struggled over benches and tried to reach Dita, but someone grabbed her by the hand and pulled her into the dance. Streamers fluttered into her face as she skipped, stumbled, galloped and stared. Where was Dita? she kept thinking. Where was she? What stupid thing had she got up to now?

Maybe she was outside. Waiting for *her*.

Becca broke free of the dancers and moved towards the gate.

But Dita wasn't there either.

Becca stood behind the gate, checking each group that left. Outside in the road, car doors were slammed and engines were started. Soon the field was almost empty, except for a few players in costume drifting around with cans of beer.

The hardboard castle began to be taken apart. The little flags trailed mournfully across the grass and a stray balloon went *splat!*

Suddenly Becca saw her.

"Dita!" she yelled. She was furious. That stupid emmet just wanted the Foolish Knight's autograph. "Dita!" she shouted. But Dita didn't seem to hear.

She tried something else. "Daisie!" Maybe Dita was still playing the part.

Dita looked across and seemed to see her. Then she turned away.

Becca wondered what to do next. She wasn't going to barge into Dita's selfish conversation with the Foolish Knight. Let her find her own way back to the house, then. And if she got lost, who cared?

Not Becca. Becca would be delighted.

But then Daisie would turn up at six, and those two had to swap clothes...

Reluctantly, she ran halfway across the field. "Dita!" she yelled. "I'm going home! Now!" She went back outside and hid behind the gate, squatting in the long grass and snapping heads off flowers, wishing each head was Dita's.

"Sorry." Dita suddenly appeared, breathless, twisting her fingers.

"You selfish pig!" exploded Becca.

"I'm *really* sorry." Dita's voice was small, subdued. "Look. I'll tell you about it one day and then you'll understand."

"Tell me about what?" snapped Becca.

Dita gulped. "Nothing much..."

They marched back to the house in silence.

I'm just being used, Becca kept thinking. *And I don't like it.*

Becca's mum was out, mowing the front lawn.

"Was it good?" she asked.

"Brilliant!" said Dita.

"Boring," Becca grumped.

They went up to Becca's room.

"I'm really sorry," repeated Dita.

"I don't care!" shouted Becca.

They sat hating each other.

"Got a chess game?" Dita said at last. "It would pass the time until Daisie gets back."

Reluctantly, Becca dug out an old chess set from the games box. "I can't play," she said.

"I'll teach you," said Dita. "Look, this is how you set out the pieces..."

Half an hour later, the bedroom door was pushed open.

"Daisie!" shrieked Dita. She ran over and hugged her.

"We did it!" they yelled, jumping and leaping. "We did it! We did it!"

Becca felt like hitting them. "I'm calling Mum," she threatened. "She'd really enjoy meeting the two of you."

The two girls jumped on her.

"You wouldn't!"

"That's mean!"

Becca struggled free. She opened the door.

"Mum!" she called.

Daisie pulled her back inside. "I'll never speak to you again if you do that," she hissed.

And those were the last words Becca would remember her saying.

Never. Speak to you. Again.

"OK, OK, I didn't mean it," said Becca. "Mum's in the garden anyway. She wouldn't have heard. But I'm out of the game from now on. Don't ask me to do a thing for you two, because I won't."

And you're not my best friend any more, Daisie Trevelyan, she added silently. *You're hers.*

CHAPTER ELEVEN

Just after lunch the next day, the telephone rang.

Becca's mum picked it up. "No," she said. "She's not with us." She called out to Becca. "Seen Daisie Trevelyan?"

"No," said Becca.

"Were you planning to meet her this afternoon?"

"I do have other friends," said Becca coldly.

"Sorry," said Mum into the phone. "Becca's not seen her, and they weren't planning anything." She turned back to Becca. "Daisie didn't turn up for lunch," she said. "Any idea where she might be? Her mum's a bit worried."

Becca nearly told her, "Over at Dita's." Then she stopped herself. She *had* promised.

"No," she said. "I haven't." Maybe Daisie'd picked up some of that girl's selfishness, she thought. Scaring her mum, when all she had to do was phone. That was thoughtless. That was mean.

New summer visitors arrived that day – two ancient, white-haired sisters who'd come down on the coach. Mum fussed over them, spreading out the guide books and making them tea.

Bet those two won't go trekking over Bodmin, like the Grahams, thought Becca. They'll hang around the whole time, wanting cups of tea and cakes.

"OK if I go swimming?" she asked. "Over in the Sports Centre."

"As long as you're back by six," said Mum.

The sisters nodded approvingly.

"Can't be too careful these days," said one.

"The things you read in the papers," sighed the second, biting delicately into her custard cream.

They were rather sweet, thought Becca grudgingly as she cycled up the road. The way old-fashioned grannies were supposed to be.

She chained her bike to a post and joined the queue for the pool. Inside, she spotted Cathie with some other girls from her class.

"Hi, Becca!" Cathie called. "Where's Daisie?"

"How would I know?" asked Becca. *We're not married,* she thought crossly. *I have got other friends.*

They splashed around in the big, glass-roofed pool, swimming lengths against each other and fooling about. She ought to get to know Cathie a bit better, Becca thought. After all, next month they'd be going to the same school, catching the same bus – which went in the opposite direction from Daisie's. Life changed. People grew up. And you didn't keep the same best friend for ever...

She arrived home to find Daisie's mum and Ben sitting in the kitchen with Mum.

Daisie's mum looked up at her eagerly. "Have you seen Daisie?" she asked. Her big, freckly face looked somehow thinner than usual, and the sun picked out the grey bits in her reddish brown hair.

"No, I haven't," said Becca. "Sorry."

Then Daisie's mum began to cry, silently, her eyes wide and brimming and tears dribbling off her chin and making a damp place on her dress. "What shall I do?" she kept saying, like some little kid.

Becca was horrified. She'd never seen a grown-up cry, except on the telly, and that wasn't real.

"Daisie'll be all right," she said awkwardly. "She's probably gone to some friend's house and forgotten the time."

Daisie's mum brightened a little. "Maybe that new girl – the one with the posh voice that Daisie kept imitating..." Then her face fell.

"But we've never met her. Don't even know her number."

Becca couldn't bear it any longer.

"I do," she said. Too bad if she gave the game away now. Daisie should have thought of that sooner.

She went over to the phone and dialled Dita's number.

"Yes?" It was Inga.

"Can I speak to Perdita?" asked Becca.

"Perdeeta in bath," said Inga.

"Please. It's urgent."

"Urgent?" Inga laughed. "Ja, ja. You kids have crush on some boy. Some pop star. I know." Becca could hear her marching away, yelling, "Deeta! Phone! Wrap up warm!"

Becca waited.

"Hi!" said Dita suddenly.

"It's Becca. Has Daisie been with you?"

"No," Dita said.

"Did you two do a swap earlier on?"

"Daisie may have," said Dita. "I mean, she's got some of my clothes and I've got some of hers. We do it whenever we feel like it. So what?" She sneezed loudly. "Listen, it's cold and I'm dripping. Why d'you want to know?"

"Because..." Becca was reluctant to put it into words. Then, "Daisie's gone missing," she said.

Becca couldn't sleep that night.

She kept remembering Dad taking Daisie's mum to the police station. Just a sensible precaution, he'd called it. It didn't mean anything really bad had happened to Daisie.

Becca had played tiddlywinks with Ben to keep him amused. "Daisie's OK really," he'd kept asking them. "Isn't she?"

"I'm sure she's OK," Mum had said comfortingly. "The policemen will help us find her. They're good at things like that."

Becca lay there in the dark, playing a scary game of what-if?

What if Daisie had drowned before she'd ever got to Dita's? The tide came in quickly around Smugglers Cove point.

Never. Speak to you. Again.

But Daisie was no emmet, Becca reminded herself. Daisie knew about tides. They all knew about tides.

What if she'd slipped on the rocks, then, and hurt herself badly? But Daisie was a champion screamer. She'd have yelled, and someone would have heard her.

What if she'd been raped? Yuk!

What if she'd been murdered? But who would murder Daisie?

And what if Becca had somehow *made* it happen by saying Daisie wasn't her best friend any more? A sort of black magic, like walking on the lines between the paving stones.

Never. Speak to you. Again.

I didn't mean it, she repeated miserably. *Oh, Daisie, please, please come back...*

Morning whitened the net curtains. The milkman chinked his bottles, and Cleo padded up and down on the duvet, like she always did.

It had been a dream, thought Becca. It wasn't really true.

But when she went downstairs, she saw Mum's grim face.

"Any news?" asked Becca, already knowing the answer.

Mum gave her a hug. "They want you and me to go to the police station," she said. "They'd like a few words with you. Don't worry, love; I'll be there." She picked up the breakfast tray for the two old ladies. "I'll have to tell them about Daisie," she sighed. "If they don't already know..."

Dita rang.

"Any news?"

"No," said Becca.

"But it's awful," wailed Dita. "What can we do?"

"I'm seeing the police this afternoon," said Becca harshly. "And I'm telling them about you. Giving them your number."

"It's supposed to be ex-directory," said Dita.

"Are you fussing?" yelled Becca. "When Daisie might be dead?"

"No," said Dita humbly. "I'm not."

Dita put the phone down shakily and walked out on to the beach. Daisie'd been special. Not just her reflection. Her friend.

She stood, watching the small waves darkening the sand. Her best friend, she thought. Her twin.

Daisie vanished? It felt like losing a bit of herself.

Daisie missing? Raped? Murdered? Like some girl in a newspaper story?

"No," said Dita fiercely. "No."

CHAPTER TWELVE

Inga hurried down to the water's edge.

"You stay with me now," she ordered, her skirt flapping in the wind. She pointed at the helicopter circling over the cliffs. "There is girl missing. Same age as you. Some crazy man, maybe sex maniac..."

"He wouldn't bother with me, then," said Dita as they walked back to the house.

"That is stupid talk," said Inga. "Put on jacket. We go out."

"If you like," said Perdita listlessly.

They drove out along the main road, then turned seaward to Zennor. Inga handed her a leaflet. "A good museum here," she announced. "Look at photos. We visit, yes?"

"If you want to," said Perdita.

They parked the car and got out. Dita followed Inga dumbly. What did room-sets of long ago farm kitchens matter? Daisie, missing, she kept thinking. Daisie. Dead.

A woman in front of them turned, then stared. She nudged her friend.

"Isn't that..?"

Dita grabbed Inga's elbow. "I feel sick," she said. "Let's go."

Behind them, she could hear the woman saying, "Looks just like Jo Trevelyan's girl – the one who's gone missing…"

"Quick!" urged Dita. "Or I'll throw up!"

On the way back, she told Inga about Daisie.

"One of your new friends the girl who is missing?" Inga gasped. "But that is awful." She touched Dita's knee. "You must be very sad."

"And she looked just like me," went on Dita. "She was my double. We played tricks on people."

"Not me," boasted Inga. "Never me." She frowned. "Double? You mean, twice times?"

Dita nodded. "Like twins…"

Inga struggled to work it out.

"But your mother not have twins, Perdeeta," she said.

There was a policewoman waiting for them when they got back.

She smiled at Perdita. "Hullo." Then she checked on a small plastic folder with two photographs inside. "You really *are* like Daisie Trevelyan, aren't you?" She spoke into

80

her radio. "Cancel lead on Scandinavian female with young girl," she said. "Girl looks like victim, but isn't."

Dita began trembling. "Victim?"

The policewoman shrugged. "Just a way of speaking," she said briskly. "Doesn't mean anything. After all, we haven't found your friend yet, have we?"

Their new neighbours hovered sympathetically, eyeing the police car. "Burglars already?" they asked.

The policewoman pointed at the front door. "I think we should talk inside, don't you?"

Inga opened a packet of biscuits and made them all tea.

The policewoman turned to Perdita. "You aren't *really* doubles, you know," she said. "Only identical twins can be doubles. But I can see what your friend meant. You do look alike." She checked again on the photos. "Very alike. Might you be related?"

Dita shook her head. "But she was my best friend."

"*Is* your best friend," corrected the policewoman. "No one's found anything yet, so we must all hope."

They talked about the games they'd played and the day Daisie had gone to St Ives with Inga.

"Not true!" protested Inga. Then she nodded. "That girl different. I notice." She nudged Dita and grinned. "She much nicer than you."

"Everyone is," said Dita miserably.

"There's that show at Tregennack," said the policewoman thoughtfully.

"It ends today," said Dita. Poor little Ben, she remembered. He'd really wanted to go.

"We must have a word with that lot," said the policewoman. "They're probably OK, but they are strangers, travellers…"

"So what?" snapped Dita. "Does that mean they're bad?"

The policewoman looked at her sharply. "Do you know them, then?"

"I went to that show," said Dita. "With Becca Hughes. On Thursday."

The policewoman pointed at Dita's Rolex. "Were you wearing that at the time?"

"Why not?" asked Dita. "It's mine."

"Not a very bright idea," said the policewoman, "showing off a watch as expensive as that."

"I wasn't showing it off!" shouted Dita.

"Perdeeta!" Inga was shocked. "This is police. Remember?"

The policewoman got up. "Don't worry," she said. "No one expects good manners at a time like this."

Just after six that evening, Liz rang.

"How's my stylish daughter?"

"OK," lied Dita.

"And what have you been up to, you and Inga?"

"Oh, nothing much. You know – museums and things. I went to the theatre on Thursday."

"Ah, the Minnack," said Liz. "Shakespeare. Which play?"

"Er – *Romeo and Juliet*." It was the only Shakespeare play she could think of.

"Good. I was hoping Inga would take you." Liz paused to light a cigarette. "Listen, sweetie – things are working out quite nicely at this end. I flew home and sorted out the flat, and it's no big problem. The burglars took the video and the computer – well, they always do! – and grabbed a few of our old tapes – too mean to buy their own, I suppose – but that was all. I took the day off when I got back here – popped over the Italian border to Lake Maggiore ... lovely!" She sighed. "So I returned to the battle refreshed, and guess what? I think I'm winning. They look as if they might be ready to sign on the dotted line. So I may be with you over there before the end of next week."

"Great," said Dita flatly.

Liz laughed. "You don't sound very enthusiastic. What have you been getting up to?"

"Nothing," Dita said.

"With your new friends? Your cats? Your dogs? Your terrapins?"

"Just mucking about."

"OK, my darling," said Liz. "Question time over. Let me have a quick word with Inga."

Dita put her hand over the phone. "Don't tell her," she whispered.

"But I must."

"Please," said Dita. "She'll only worry and come rushing down early. And she's got very important business to do."

And how easy it would be, she thought (listening to Inga's reassuring, "Fine, fine, Miss Powell. Everything fine. No problems") for Perdita Powell to vanish for ever and Daisie Trevelyan to be found. She'd fooled Daisie's mum already. She could do it again.

She'd soon pick up a Cornish accent. And the kittens would be hers then, and so would Drac.

But what if Daisie turned up?

She was suddenly shocked by the idea. It was like stealing someone's life. Her best friend's life. She didn't know why she'd dreamed it up in the first place. Unless she really *was* bad, as Becca seemed to think.

The Rolex glittered on her wrist. Supposing someone *had* spotted it and tried to steal it? Mistaken Daisie for her? It made sense, didn't it? The policewoman had seen that.

Her fault again, she thought...

Inga said goodbye to Liz.

"I not tell. You hear?" she said, putting down the phone. She frowned at Dita. "You are sad for your friend. We go to cinema, yes? Will cheer you up."

But Dita shook her head. The prospect of a film would have seemed fun a few days ago, but not now.

She went outside and sat on the terrace, watching the evening sun bronzing the waves and the gulls swooping and strutting along the darkening beach. The first star began twinkling between the clouds.

What was out there, wondered Dita.

God?

Daisie?

Later that evening, the phone rang again.

"If it's Becca," shouted Dita, "then call me."

She heard Inga's voice, disdainful, off-putting. "Yes... What shock?... What wrong name?... Miss Powell in *Switzerland*... This afternoon. A police lady. Very nice. No hassle... Not tonight, it is too late... No!" Inga sighed hugely. "If you wish, but it is not necessary..."

"Whoever was that?" asked Dita.

"Oh, you know." Inga's lips curled in distaste, as if she'd just tasted something nasty. "Him. The estate man."

"Tweetie Pie? At this time?"

"He was in pub, I think," said Inga. "I hear lots of noise. A little drunk, I would say –

stupid man. Talk nonsense. Ask if your mother is here. I tell him no. Then he ask to come and see me now. Thinks I am alone when I am au pair." She pulled a face. "He mad."

"So what did you tell him?"

Inga shrugged. "What do you think?"

"I'm going to bed anyway," pointed out Dita. "So you *will* be alone." She giggled. "Lover Boy could have you all to himself..."

Inga threw a cushion at her. "Bad girl!" she said. She began marching about, doing up locks and checking the alarm. "We leave on some lights, OK?"

"Oh, Inga," said Dita. "Stop fussing!"

"Bad man out there," said Inga. "Steal children."

"We are *not* children," protested Dita.

"OK. Young ladies..." Inga switched off the TV. "So he come round tomorrow. Just to check, he say. Ja."

"Who? The sex maniac?"

"Mister Sparrow. I *tell* you."

"You mean, old Tweetie Pie?"

Inga nodded.

"To check on what?" asked Dita. Then she grinned and pointed. "Oh, Inga," she said. "He means *you*."

CHAPTER THIRTEEN

Becca woke up early, even though it was Sunday. She kept hearing people outside in the road.

"What's going on?" she asked Mum at breakfast.

"They've all come to help," explained Mum, "in the search for Daisie. Your dad's out there, too. And Daisie's dad's come down."

"Shouldn't we help, then?" asked Becca. She wanted to be out there, doing something. Anything.

"They've got as many people as they can manage," said Mum. "Anyway, you're too young."

Becca was offended. "Who says so?"

"The police."

"Well, that's stupid," said Becca. "Daisie's my best friend. Anyway, young people are better at picking up clues."

The phone rang.

"It's that girl again," said Mum.

"She *has* got a name." Becca took the phone. "Hi, *Perdita!*" she said, scowling at Mum.

"Any news?"

"They're out searching along the lane and in the fields," said Becca grimly. "Masses of them. There's a helicopter, too."

"I know," said Dita. "I can hear it." She paused. "Listen – can you come over?"

"Are you joking?" asked Becca. "They've put a twenty-four hour guard on me!"

"Get your dad to drive you, then."

"Dad's out helping with the search."

"Your mum, then." Dita paused. "Something's come up. It's important. We need to talk."

Becca imagined how it would feel, seeing Daisie's face on the wrong girl. "I couldn't bear to," she said. "You know why."

"It's about Daisie," urged Dita. "Something someone said."

Becca was irritated. "Then tell me now," she said. "Or tell the police."

"I need *you*," said Perdita. "Please."

Becca turned to Mum. "Perdita's asked me over…"

"No way," said Mum firmly.

"You could drive me," said Becca. "And pick me up afterwards."

Mum considered it. "Maybe it's not such a

88

bad idea," she said slowly. "It's a lovely day. Get you away from all this. Do you good."

Becca thought of something else. "We could pick up Drac," she suggested. "He must be really miserable without Daisie."

Mum hugged her and said weepily, "You *are* a nice girl."

"Hey," said Becca, squirming. "It's Daisie who's missing, you know. Not me."

They found Daisie's mum being comforted by neighbours.

"I'm going over to Smugglers Cove," said Becca, embarrassed. "To see Daisie's friend Perdita. I could take Drac if you like."

"Oh, take him," said Daisie's mum, her hair all tangled and her face streaked with tears. "He's done nothing but pine since she left, poor beast."

Becca's mum stepped forward and touched her shoulder. "Daisie'll turn up, Joanna," she said. "Kids do."

But Daisie's mum just turned her face away.

"Alive?" she asked bitterly. "Injured? Raped? Or dead?"

Drac curled up immediately on the back seat of the car. His sad brown eyes rested for a moment on Becca's face, as if she might have the answer. Then he whimpered and closed them.

They parked above Smugglers Cove and walked down to the houses. Mum gawped at the palms and the burglar alarm boxes. "These people must be made of money," she sniffed.

Drac ran inside when Inga opened the door.

"Oh, Drac!" they heard Dita yelling. "Oh, Draccie!"

Mum gave Inga a hard look. "I'm Mrs Hughes," she announced. "Rebecca's mother."

"Ah." Inga smiled at Becca. "You are the other girl, then? You do not look like Perdeeta."

"How long can she stay?" asked Becca's mum. "She needs to come home for lunch."

"She can eat with us," invited Inga. "No problem."

"In that case, I'll pick her up at about three," said Becca's mum, following Inga into the lounge. "Is that convenient?" She suddenly caught sight of Dita playing with Drac. "I don't believe it," she gasped, clutching the wall.

"They're doubles," said Becca. "I *did* tell you."

"Well, don't ever let Daisie's lot see her," said Mum. "If something bad's happened to Daisie, it would kill them."

It's almost killing me, thought Becca. *It's awful. It's wrong. She shouldn't look so much like Daisie.*

"It's not my fault." It was as if Dita had read her thoughts. "I can't help looking like her, can I?" Then Dita burst into tears.

90

Becca ran across and put an arm around her shoulders. "Let's go down to the beach," she said. "Then we can talk."

"We can talk in here," sniffled Dita.

"Well, I must be going," said Becca's mum awkwardly. She turned to Inga. "You *will* watch them, won't you?"

"Is my job," said Inga stiffly, seeing Mum out.

As soon as the girls were settled, Drac jumped into Dita's lap and began licking her damp cheeks.

Inga came back. "You two no go to beach?"

"We want to talk," announced Dita. "To you, too."

"To me?" Inga sat down in an armchair and crossed her legs. "OK. So talk."

"What time is Tweetie Pie coming?"

"Mr Sparrow? He say one o'clock." Inga fiddled with an earring. "If he remember. He was drunk last night. He say stupid things…"

"What things?" demanded Dita.

Inga shrugged. "I tell you already."

"Tell both of us," said Dita.

Inga frowned. "He think your mother is here," she said, counting on her fingers. "He think I have shock. And yes, he say the radio make mistake over the name of your friend…"

"Why would he think that?"

"Like I tell you," said Inga. "He drunk. Mad, maybe. And he wish to visit me. At that

91

time. Maybe he think you are in bed already."
She grinned. "That man know nothing about
eleven-year-old girls."

"Maybe he thought I wasn't around."

Inga looked shocked. "He think I am not
responsible?"

"No, Inga," said Becca slowly. "Maybe he
expected *Dita* to be missing."

Dita nodded excitedly. "And that's why he
said they got the name wrong."

"You mean, someone take that other girl?"
said Inga. "Think she is you?"

"But why would anyone pick on Dita?"
asked Becca.

"My Rolex, for one thing," said Dita,
waving her wrist. "But they wouldn't want me
to go with it."

Inga uncrossed her legs and walked over to
the kitchen. "Perdeeta's mother has money,"
she said, coming back with orange juice and
three glasses on a tray. "Maybe somebody
know that..." The ice cubes crackled as she
poured out three drinks. "Mr Sparrow must
know that – rent for this house big money."
Inga frowned. "He also knew that police had
been here. But no reason for police to be here.
Dita is not missing. They only came here
because of that woman in the museum."

"They'd have turned up anyway," corrected
Becca. "They're looking for clues. They talked
to me, too. They're talking to all Daisie's

friends." She suddenly remembered something. "But Tweetie Pie doesn't know you're her friend, does he?"

"You see?" Dita's eyes were shining. "It fits."

"He *knows* something," shouted Becca. "Quick. Let's ring the police!"

But Dita shook her head. "Not yet. I want us to trap him."

"How?"

Dita grinned. "We'll scare him." She turned to Inga. "When he turns up, you must pretend that I *am* missing."

Inga looked sheepish. "I no good actor."

"You've got to be," said Dita. "It's important. Daisie might be dead."

"There *are* people around," pointed out Becca. "People who've seen you already."

Dita shrugged. "You mean, our neighbours? They'll play. Inga can tell them the police have asked us to set this up." She grinned. "They'll love it."

"Dita, you're amazing!" said Becca admiringly.

"There's more. When he leaves, I'll be waiting for him in the car park." Dita giggled. "If he's done something to Daisie, he'll flip! He'll think he's seeing a ghost!"

Becca shuddered. Only dead people had ghosts. "So what about me?" she asked. "What do I do?"

"Oh, don't you see?" Dita's voice was almost squeaky. "You're our prime *witness*. If Tweetie Pie gives himself away, and then afterwards tries to claim Inga got things wrong, we'll have *you*, won't we? And Tweetie Pie doesn't know you. He'll think you're just some kid on the beach, if he sees you at all." She stared at Becca. "He won't know that you're our listener, our super-spy."

Becca looked doubtful. "So where am I supposed to be doing all this?"

"No problem." Inga was in charge now. "I make sandwiches. You girls eat quickly, then go out." She picked up a portable telephone and threw it into Dita's lap. "You take this when you hide in car park. You call me if you have trouble."

"Trouble?" Dita sniggered. "With that little wimp?"

"But what about me?" persisted Becca.

"You sit on rocks down there. Read a magazine – I give you. You listen."

Inga stroked back her hair. "I take Mister Tweetie Pie on to terrace. Give him coffee and big Swedish sandwich – ja. We talk." She smiled and nodded. "We talk a lot!"

CHAPTER FOURTEEN

The two girls scrambled down to the flat rocks just below the terrace.

Perdita checked on the time. "Another ten minutes," she said. She looked at Becca. "When he gets here, you take Drac, and I'll climb round the back of the car park and hide. You wait here and pick up all you can."

Becca nodded. "What then?"

Dita was working it out. "When you hear him leaving," she said, "you just stroll up after him. You know, as if you were going to get something from your parents' car – beach towel, sandwiches..."

"Wish that last bit was true," sighed Becca. "I'm still hungry."

"Too bad."

"So what then? I mean, when I get to the car park."

"You call out," said Dita. She grinned. "You yell. Then we get him!"

They heard a car moving down the private road. They heard tyres scraping gravel, then silence.

They looked at each other. "Him?" they mouthed.

They heard the brief bleep of an alarm. Becca stood up to look, then she ducked down.

"Someone's walking down the path," she whispered, "but I can't see who."

They strained to hear something against the hiss of the waves. Somewhere on the beach, a little kid began yelling. "S-s-s-sh," they breathed. "S-s-s-sh!"

Then, from somewhere above their heads they heard Inga's voice, loud, fakey, enthusiastic. "Oh, Meester Sparrow! Is so nice to see you."

And a man: "Nick, please." A pause. "How awful… Her mother…"

A couple of gulls began swooping and squabbling. *Oh, shut up!* thought Becca. *Shut up!*

"…coming down soon, I would think…" The front door slammed on the rest of his words.

"What now?" whispered Becca.

"Just wait. Inga'll work on him, get him out on the terrace. He's got a thing about her." Dita looked suddenly grim. "He *does* know something, doesn't he?" She got up. "OK. I'm off."

Drac whimpered, struggling to follow her, but Becca held him. "Stay!" she said fiercely, trying to sound as bossy as Daisie.

She watched Dita scrambling up the rocks that flanked the back of the house and running across the grassy slope above the car park. Then she ducked into the bushes and Becca lost her.

A man in a blue jumper and jeans came strolling along the beach. Becca spread open her magazine and watched him over the pages.

The man hung around, looking up at the houses. Then he seemed to spot Becca.

She heard him crunching towards her over the pebbles and rocks.

"Excuse me," he said, and Drac began to bark.

Becca looked up at the man. He had a short, broad nose, a funny, curly mouth and thick dark brows that looked all wrong with grey hair.

"Aren't you Perdita's friend?" he asked. "Didn't I see you at the show?"

"Oh, no," said Becca quickly. This guy was a nuisance. If he really knew Dita, he could come back some other time. "Who's Perdita?" she asked cleverly.

"...girl of about your age," shouted the man above Drac's din. "With a nanny or something. Staying in one of those houses, but I'm not sure which." He danced about, dodging Drac. "Can't you shut your dog up?"

Becca heard people coming out on to the terrace. This clown would ruin everything. She *had* to get rid of him.

"Drac's my guard dog," she said rudely. "And you're upsetting him."

"I am?" The man ruffled Drac's ears. "Sorry," he said.

Becca glowered. "Watch it. He bites."

"OK, OK," grinned the man. "I can take a hint."

Becca watched him moving over the rocks, hesitating, looking back at the houses, then climbing up to the slope, the way Dita had gone. He knew something, too, she thought.

Suddenly she felt scared. What if that was *him*? The bloke who'd taken Daisie? Maybe he was a friend of Tweetie Pie's – a robber, a sex maniac. Maybe they were working together. It wasn't hard to twist that face into something evil – that iron grey hair caught back in a ponytail, that single gold earring, those dark, heavy brows like something from a horror film...

She snapped out of it and concentrated on listening again. Watching and listening were what she was there for. Like a super-spy, she reminded herself. Like a super-detective, a private eye.

"Nice weather, for a change..." That was *his* voice. Chairs scraped against tiles, and plates or glasses clinked against a hard surface. "...Swedish sandwiches," he was drooling. "I really go for things Scandinavian, you may have noticed that already... " (What a wally! thought Becca) "... deserve a bottle of wine. I'll nip down to the Off Licence..."

"For you only, then." That was Inga. "I do not drink."

"And it shows," said Tweetie Pie. "That luscious Swedish skin..."

Becca heard a small commotion, then Inga's voice, sharp, angry. "I not like to be touched..." She hesitated. "Not now."

Clever Inga, thought Becca, leading him on.

"Sorry..." That was Tweetie Pie. "You're upset. It's understandable..." Then the gulls made a din again and blanked out his words.

Did she have enough information? wondered Becca. Tweetie Pie was clearly going on as if something had happened.

"...one child missing," wailed Inga loudly. "And now my little Per-dee-ta." She gave a theatrical sob. "Gone!"

Becca clapped her hand over her mouth to stop herself laughing. Inga'd trapped him! She was brilliant! And she said she couldn't act.

"...take you out for a drive. Get you away from all this..."

"Oh, no!" Inga sounded shocked now. "My

duty is here."

"Then I'll stay with you…"

"The police," Inga squeaked. "They come soon. I must not have a man with me." Her voice dropped. "You come later, Nick," she suggested. "This evening, no?"

The chairs scraped again. Becca got up. Tweetie Pie would be out soon. She wandered over to the path, stopping to pick up a pebble or a shell (Inga wasn't the only one who could act, she thought).

Released, Drac scampered over the rocks, barking wildly at gulls. Then he dived into the bushes and disappeared.

"Drac!" called Becca nervously. "Come out of there!" She felt safer with a dog, even if he *was* small. "Drac!" she yelled, and Drac emerged reluctantly, his fur speckled with yellow petals. "Heel!" Becca ordered, and, "Stay close!" and to her amazement, Drac obeyed.

She hung about, throwing pebbles for Drac and waiting for someone to come out of the house. What would he look like, this Tweetie Pie? Dark, Becca guessed, and oily. With a smarmy suit and flashy tie and chunky gold rings.

A bouncy, mousy-haired man in a neat blue shirt, a blazer and grey cotton pants stepped out smartly in front of her. He paused, and called back, "See you later, Inga…"

Becca gawped at him, amazed. Was that him?

Then he really *was* a Tweetie Pie.

She stopped being scared. No wonder Dita'd acted so brave. He looked just like Mr Davies, the school caretaker. Mr Davies was short and bossy, always ordering people about, but who was afraid of old Mavis Davies?

She skipped boldly round in front of him, then deliberately held back, pretending to examine a fern or a flower.

Wait till they got him in the car park, she gloated. Then they'd fix him!

Hanging back, she followed him in. That beat-up green sports car was his, she decided, but Tweetie Pie began fiddling with the back doors of a van.

This was it, thought Becca. Action!

"Dita!" she yelled.

And Dita came leaping out of the bushes and Drac went crazy, galloping up to her.

"Hullo, Mr Sparrow," Dita called, waving her portable phone.

Tweetie Pie turned, froze. "You..." Becca heard him choke. Then Drac was kicked out of the way, the phone smashed against the ground and Dita grabbed, pushed, and slammed inside the van.

A second man came shouting down the hill, but the van's engine roared, cutting out his voice. Tyres skidded on gravel, and Becca caught a glimpse of someone leaping, running, and through the windscreen of the van, Tweetie Pie's white face behind a swinging car toy, like something in a goldfish bowl, mouth grimly open, eyes fixed and staring, before he swung the van round and squealed into the road. Drac staggered forward, trying to follow it. Then he stood there, dazed.

Becca snatched him up. "Poor old vampire," she muttered. "You did your best…"

She snapped out of shock as the second man moved in on them. She started to run, but a tree root tripped her. She screamed as the man lifted her into the sports car.

"Belt up!" he ordered as he got in beside her.

Then a cloud of dust gagged her as they squealed away.

CHAPTER FIFTEEN

"Belt up," repeated the man. "And keep that dog off me."

Becca glanced quickly at the iron grey pony-tail and the heavy brows, the gold earring and the blue jumper and jeans. It was the man from the beach. So he *was* working with Tweetie Pie.

"Drac's a vampire," she threatened foolishly. "And if he bites you, you'll die."

The man reached across. "*You'll* die," he warned her, fastening her seat belt.

They followed the van into the main road. So she'd guessed right, Becca thought. He *had* been up to something. "You two won't get away with it," she shouted. "Inga knows everything. She's rung the police!"

The man nodded calmly. "So what do *you* know?"

"Me?" Becca was baffled. "Everything, too," she said weakly. "Same as Inga." He *is* a

103

maniac, she thought. He's not even bothered.

The man looked at her. "Then tell me."

"Tell you what?" A tractor moved past them on the other side of the road and Becca screamed at the driver. "Help me! Help!"

The man slapped her on the cheek. "Do you want to see your friend alive?"

Becca nodded dumbly.

"Then shut up." He signalled left. "And tell me," he insisted, slowing down.

"Find out for yourself," spat Becca, as they turned after the van. "I'm not going to help you two."

The man paused. "Do you hate Dita so much?"

"Hate Dita?" He *was* mad, she thought again. "I don't hate Dita."

"I saw that police poster, you see," the man said, almost to himself. "It looked so much like her. I was worried…" He was quiet for a while, concentrating on the road. "And now she's been taken too."

"I don't know what you're talking about," said Becca boldly.

"A second girl taken," shouted the man. "Aren't you scared?"

The vehicle in front suddenly braked, swerved, backed, then screeched off past them.

"OK. If that's what he wants," the man muttered. He reversed the sports car in a tight circle, then scraped off in a shower of earth and leaves. "We'll keep our distance this time," he said. "Make him think he's lost us. Don't want him speeding..." He glanced sideways at Becca. "Perdita may be your friend," he said, "but she's the only child I've got."

Becca gasped.

"You?" she said slowly. "Dita's *dad*?"

The man sighed. "Not a very good one. Too selfish. But I do care."

They plunged into a deep lane, dark as a tunnel, where tree roots twisted and clawed into steeply rising banks.

"Dita's dad..." repeated Becca. She suddenly remembered something. "Was it you she was talking to? After that show?"

Dita's dad smiled sadly. "The Foolish Knight? Yes, that was me."

Crossroads blinded them for a moment with silver sun and shadows. Then they dived into the darkness of another lane.

The van rounded a curve. Then it seemed to vanish. The man put his foot down. "He can't be out of sight yet," he muttered. "He'd have to drive at the speed of light."

"There was a turning back there," yelled Becca. "There was a signpost in the hedge and a sort of driveway..."

The man braked, then backed.

A battered road sign, half-hidden by leaves, said: NANTENNON 1.

"Bet that's where he's gone," said the man, turning in. "Like a rat into a hole...."

A little way down, they saw a big sign mounted on wooden posts.

MERLIN'S HIDEAWAY, it read. SIX LUXURY HOMES BY GUINEVERE DEVELOPMENTS. And underneath: PRIVATE PROPERTY. NO PUBLIC ACCESS TO BEACH. And below that: WARNING. GUARD DOGS LOOSE ON SITE.

Dita's dad pulled up and got out. He examined the sign, then stepped cautiously past it and began walking down the road. Becca huddled, shivering, in the open-topped car, cuddling Drac and listening for the guard dogs.

For a moment, Dita's dad seemed to drop out of sight. Then he turned and came back. Drac wriggled free and ran up to him, leaping and barking.

"Hey, what's all this? Are you one of the guard dogs?" Dita's dad scooped Drac up and walked back to the car.

"I think their hounds must be having Sunday off," he said. "Or maybe they only patrol at night. But you were right. The van's down there, along with another car. They're both parked outside the show house." He dumped Drac on to Becca and got in, slamming the door. "Take good care of your mistress, vampire," he said, turning on the engine. "I should never have picked her up."

He backed slowly out of the track and into

the lane. Then he turned down to the cross-roads and pulled in on the grass.

"But we *know* Dita's there," argued Becca. The man nodded.

"But we don't want him to know that we're here too..." He opened the car door. "I'm going to have a closer look at that show house," he said.

"Great!" said Becca. "After all, we've got Drac."

They walked back up the lane and stopped at the opening.

"No further," said the man. "I'll do this alone. And I want you to get away from here. Quickly. It's too dangerous. Walk up the lane, and keep on walking until you find a house, a caravan, people, somebody. Get them to ring the police. Tell them, Nantennon."

Becca looked up at him. It was a nice face, a sad clown's face, the face in Dita's photograph.

"Please let me come with you," she begged. "They don't want me. And that man might hurt you. Anyway, it's not just Dita down there. It could be Daisie."

Dita's dad looked puzzled. "Who's Daisie?"

"The other girl. The girl who's really missing. She's Dita's double. And she's my best friend."

"Dita's *double*? Then that would explain..."

Becca nodded. "Inga thinks they took Daisie instead of Dita."

"Inga?"

"The au pair."

"Well, it does fit." The man shook his head. "Perdita'd be worth something in ransom money. But the answer's still no, madam. I can take care of myself, even without your vampire." He touched Becca's shoulder and smiled down at her. "My daughter's friend," he said gently. "And I don't even know your name."

"Rebecca Hughes," said Becca primly. Then she grinned. "Becca."

Dita's dad held out his hand. "Martin Fitzpatrick. A truly Foolish Knight." His eyes were Daisie's eyes, Dita's eyes. "Good luck, Becca!" he said. "We're all depending on you!"

Becca walked back along the path, Drac trotting at her heels. Why did everyone, she wondered, have to depend on her?

She turned left and walked on up the road. Her legs still felt trembly. The road climbed slowly into open country. There had to be a house somewhere, Becca thought. Those cows had to belong to someone...

She came to another crossroads and turned down towards the sea. There might be caravans, she told herself, families out on a picnic, emmets, she thought. Even an emmet would do.

A single car came into sight along the empty road. Becca shot out her hand and it slowed and pulled in.

The window slid down and a woman glared at her. "Hitch-hiking at your age?" she bellowed. "Dangerous. Where's your mother?"

Becca ran up to her. "Oh, please," she begged. "Have you got a phone?"

A man leaned over. "Kid's after something," he said. "Car phones, most likely…" The window slid up and they moved away.

Then Becca began to cry, big hot tears that dribbled salt. She was lost. She was frightened. And there was no one to help.

And Martin might have been hurt by now. Murdered. Along with Daisie and Dita…

Drac smelt a rabbit. His legs stiffened as he savoured its scent. Then he bounded into the bracken.

"Drac!" sobbed Becca. "Come here!" But her voice kept breaking.

She ran across the clifftops, calling him. "Drac! Drac!"

The little tracks zigzagged through gorse and ferns. "Drac!" gasped Becca. "I'll kill you! I'll kill you!"

The rabbit paths dipped and swerved, following the contours of the cliffs. Below, on her right, the sea glittered and faded.

"Drac!" Becca shrieked.

If she climbed back to the road, he might follow, she thought.

Or he might not.

The thought of going on without Drac was too frightening. "Drac!" she called again, scrambling down.

Then she saw them. The houses. Nestling in a valley near a little beach.

She lowered herself down to the level of the rocks. Gulls dipped and squabbled, then circled out to sea. Drac didn't matter now, only the houses.

Her legs scratched and bleeding, she ran down a wider track between rocks and hill grass, found a dry stone wall half-covered in rock rose, scrambled over a stile next to a rusty sign: FOOTPATH, then followed another track through bushes and came out on a beach.

She picked her way between rocks thickly garlanded with mussels. On her left, in the valley, the houses loomed, half-built, hollow, forbidding. In front of them a digger stood idle, its yellow jaw half-open and its metal teeth encrusted with dried mud.

It was a building site, Becca realized. She'd made a mistake.

Then she spotted a man running. He'd do, she thought. She scrabbled over the pebbles and up on to the bank.

"Hey!" she called out. "Help! *Please!*" But

the man plunged into the bushes and disappeared.

Her eyes prickled with tears. He must have heard her, she thought.

Then she turned, and her heart closed up.

On one side of the road, a sign read: SHOW HOUSE. On the other stood Tweetie Pie's van.

She was stupid. She knew now.

She'd walked in a circle.

Back to Nantennon.

CHAPTER
SIXTEEN

Something cracked through the bushes, flushing out a shower of frightened birds.

Becca froze.

Then she dropped to the ground, covering her head with her hands.

Another crack! of gunfire, then the screech of tyres on rubble as a car sped away. She heard someone crashing about over the churned-up stones. She wanted to crawl away, run, hide, but her legs wouldn't move.

She heard footsteps coming back, trudge-trudge over the ground. They stopped. She held her breath. Her heart was pounding. She felt boots brushing her side, and heard something drop with a thud. Then hands were around her, hauling her up.

She fought him, struggling, kicking, biting.

"Becca," said the man.

She dared to look at his face then, and

saw it was Martin.

He picked her up and carried her across to the house. "The rat got away," he muttered. "But at least I took his number…"

"He had a gun?" stammered Becca.

Martin nodded. "So did I."

Becca gaped at him. "You?"

"It was the woman's…" Martin gave a bitter laugh. "That guy must have known I couldn't use it."

"Where is it now?"

"I dropped it." He took her inside and set her down on a sofa. "I'll go and fetch the nasty thing," he told her. "It's loaded, and I don't want anyone else to get hurt."

Becca lay back against frilly flowered cushions. The room was shadowy, unreal, like something in a dream. Heavy Venetian blinds threw a pattern of sun-stripes over a sheepskin rug, and in front of the sofa, magazines lay scattered on a low, glass-topped table. There were screwed-up tissues on the floor, a half-smoked, red-stained cigarette stub in a heavy turquoise ash-tray, and a shiny leather hand-bag with an elaborate gold clasp slung across the back of a chair.

Two big flower prints looked down on a table messy with bottles, cans, foil take-away boxes and paper plates, and in the corner, on a trolley, a small television set was flickering and babbling. Becca picked out a voice: "And now for the jackpot!" when she heard something scrabbling on the other side of the wall.

Then a small dog came galloping across the beige carpet, leapt into Becca's lap and started licking her face.

"Drac!" said Becca, hugging him. "Oh, Drac!"

Dita came in at the same moment as Martin. When she saw Becca, she ran across and hugged her. "Oh, Becca!" she said. "You're OK! You're safe!"

Then she drew back, looking suddenly solemn.

"She's bleeding a lot," she told Martin. "And moaning." Her voice sounded wobbly. "Is she going to die?"

And Becca caught her breath. They were talking about Daisie!

"We need to get her to hospital. Quickly," said Martin. "Becca, can you stand up? We need all the help we can get."

She followed them upstairs, her heart thumping. Daisie attacked, she thought. Daisie hurt.

Martin and Dita ran into a bedroom, but Becca hung back, scared of what she might see.

"Come on!" urged Martin. "I need the two of you for Daisie." He came out cradling a woman whose left arm was trailing, whose blonde hair was matted and sticky with blood.

"You two get Daisie!" he ordered. "Stand her up and help her downstairs."

Confused, Becca followed Dita into the bedroom, and found someone lying on top of the bed.

The someone blinked sleepy eyes and smiled at Becca dreamily. "Hullo, my bird..."

"Daisie!" shrieked Becca.

"Stand her up!" shouted Martin. "Get her walking downstairs."

The two girls put their arms under Daisie's shoulders, then heaved. Daisie smiled at them soppily. "Nice work, my handsomes," she murmured, her head drooping on to Becca's chest.

Half-hauling, half-dragging, they somehow got her downstairs. Drac ran round them in circles, getting in the way.

They stumbled out of the house, following Martin.

"What happened to that woman?" asked Becca.

"He shot her."

"Martin did?"

"Don't be stupid!" Dita glared at Becca. "Listen. My dad was a hero." She sighed. "It was like something from a James Bond film..."

Martin overheard. "Don't exaggerate," he said. "And get the back of this van open."

"But that's Tweetie Pie's van," said Becca.

"Too bad." Martin set the woman gently on

the floor, covering her with an old rug. "We need the space." He waved. "Come on. Get Daisie inside." He sighed. "OK, vampire-dog, if you *have* to sit on her stomach. And now you two…" He slammed the doors and walked round to the front.

"Left his keys for us, too," he said, starting the engine.

"But where *is* Tweetie Pie?" asked Dita.

Martin shrugged. "Lying low, I should think. Ready to help out his friend. Some friend!" He hooted, then turned into the lane. "I wouldn't want to be in that guy's bad books…"

Becca was puzzled. "Which guy?"

"Tell her," Martin said to Dita. "You saw more of him than me."

"He was Tweetie Pie's boss, or something," said Dita.

"Start at the beginning," said Martin, "or she'll never understand."

"Well," Dita said. "When Tweetie Pie saw me, back in the car park, he thought I'd escaped, so he grabbed me and brought me here. He dragged me inside that house, and there they both were."

"Who?" asked Becca.

"Tweetie Pie's boss. And his rotten girl-friend." She pointed at the figure wrapped in a rug. "The minute they saw me, they started screaming at each other in Italian or something. Then she grabbed me and marched me upstairs,

116

and there was Daisie, asleep on the bed. Then the man stormed off back to Tweetie Pie, leaving *her* to guard us." Dita shivered. "She had that gun."

"So what about Daisie?" said Becca.

Daisie shifted, hearing her name. "What about Daisie?" she repeated, ruffling Drac's fur. Then she let her head fall into Becca's lap.

"They gave her some sleeping drug," whispered Dita, "to keep her quiet." She paused. "Well. We heard the two men arguing outside, Tweetie Pie going on about *twins* and *how was I to know?* and the man saying something about shutting up Inga..." She shuddered. "Then they went off in the car."

"I heard them go," said Martin. "I was skulking around in the bushes. I'd already taken down their number. Not that it'll help now – they'll probably ditch that Volvo."

Dita pointed at the woman. "Well, *she* just sat there, playing with the gun and looking at us. Then I heard someone moving about downstairs..."

"I thought they'd left," protested Martin. "I thought the coast was clear..."

"...and the bedroom door opened and there was Dad!"

"Not very impressive," said Martin. "She turned the gun on me, too." He chuckled. "It was really Becca who saved us."

"Me?"

"It was the way Drac turned up out of nowhere," said Dita. "You were brilliant, doubling back! Drac just went crazy! Jumped on the bed, then leapt up at the woman, the gun went flying and Martin just leapt on it!" She smiled proudly. "By the time Tweetie Pie's boss got back, Dad was completely in control." She reached out and touched Martin's shoulder. "Cool," she said admiringly.

"Not at the end," said Martin, shaking his head. "He got away, didn't he? He even tried to kill his girlfriend, and I was just standing there."

"Bet he guessed you didn't know how to use that thing," said Dita. "But he couldn't be sure." She grinned. "You're much too good an actor…"

They turned into the courtyard of St Mary's Hospital.

Martin ran inside, and came out with nurses and trolleys. "Daisie'll have to be looked at too," he explained. "We don't know what rubbish those people put into her."

When they'd tucked up Daisie in a red woolly blanket, Drac wriggled in beside her and snuggled down.

The nurses reached for him. "We can't have dogs in the hospital, my dear," they said.

"Then I won't go," said Daisie, opening one eye.

The nurses whispered, then nodded. "We'll pop her into a private room for a while," they told Martin. "Sister's quite understanding…"

They began pushing the trolleys.

"What's your little dog called, dear?" one of them asked.

Daisie stared at her glassily.

"Dracula," she croaked.

CHAPTER
SEVENTEEN

They drove back towards Tregennack. Dita sat with Martin, in the front of the van.

"Hey, that was our turn-off," she complained. "And you've just missed it!"

"We're not going home yet," said Martin. "We need to call in at the police station."

"But I'm starving," grumbled Dita. "Couldn't we go back for a sandwich?"

"Don't you want that man to be caught?" Martin said. "Not to mention our friend Tweetie Pie."

"I'd swap the lot of them for a hot pasty," sighed Becca from the back.

In the interview room, they found Inga with Becca's mum and dad. A policewoman stopped them all from rushing forward. "These children are still under stress," she said.

"*Children?*" screeched Dita. "I like that!"

The policewoman turned. "Sit down

quietly," she told them. She sounded just like a teacher. "And someone will bring you tea and biscuits. We might even have some sweets…"

"You wouldn't have a hot pasty, would you?" asked Becca.

"Our doctor will need to check you over…"

"Oh, those two are fine," said Martin, grinning at them. "Tough as old boots…"

Then Becca's mum came over and put her arms around Becca. "Thank God you're safe," she whispered. She gave a little sob and Becca blushed.

Inga frowned at Dita. "Your mother arrive tomorrow."

"Tomorrow?" squealed Dita. "How come? I mean, why?"

The policewoman smiled. "She rang us," she explained. "This morning. You see, your mother was being blackmailed." She spoke very slowly, as if they couldn't possibly understand. "Your mother received a fax. On Friday." She took a document out of a file. "WE HAVE YOUR DAUGHTER," she read. "GIVE UP ON THE SWISS PROJECT OR PERDITA DIES."

Dita gasped. "They were going to kill me?"

"Well, one of you," said the policewoman. "It might have been Daisie Trevelyan." She looked very hard at Martin. "And I don't believe in doubles."

"Well, I do," said Becca. "There's that lady on the telly who looks just like the Queen."

Dita was quiet for a moment, working something out. "Liz got that fax on Friday," she said. "So why didn't she ring you then?"

"She hadn't seen it," said the policewoman. "You see, the kidnappers sent it to your London address."

"But Liz was in Switzerland," said Dita. "She had to stay on."

The policewoman nodded. "The next door neighbour picked it up, and phoned it through to your mother this morning…"

"Oh, that was Maggie," said Dita. "She always checks on things." She thought of something else. "But how did the kidnappers know where to find me? Liz only tells a few people."

Martin grimaced. "And I'm not one of them."

"But your mother booked the house months ago," explained the policewoman. "The details were on her computer."

"And they steal the computer," said Inga. "Those people who burgle the flat."

"So catch one of them," said Martin, "and you might pull in the lot."

Dita sighed. "Poor Liz," she said. "She's got so much to worry about…"

"But what about Tweetie Pie?" asked Becca.

"Who?"

"Mr Sparrow. The man from Guinevere Estates."

"They must have offered him money," said the policewoman. "Big money, too, to take a risk like that. But we won't really know until we find him."

Dita frowned. "But how could Liz be sure the blackmailer wasn't just fooling? I mean, making the whole thing up?"

The policewoman looked uncomfortable. "I think I'd rather not tell you that."

"They'd send her a lock of your hair," said Martin. "And then they'd go on to other things. Fingernails, maybe. Then fingers." He was clearly enjoying himself. "Ears!"

"Ugh!" shuddered Dita. "But that man would have done it. He was evil. I saw him shoot his girlfriend, and his face didn't even change." She hesitated, not wanting to say it. "Maybe he did kill her. She looked pretty dead to me…"

CHAPTER EIGHTEEN

"We must ring the Trevelyans," said Becca's mum next day, "and find out how Daisie is."

"Can't we go in and see her?" asked Becca.

"Let's leave her in peace," said Mum. "Daisie was drugged, remember. These things take time." She dialled Daisie's number. "Tomorrow afternoon?" she exclaimed. "Aren't they rushing things a bit?"

"Tomorrow afternoon?" repeated Becca. "You mean Daisie'll be out of hospital tomorrow? Great! We'll go and see her then."

But Mum shook her head.

"Wednesday," she said firmly. "And not before."

So Becca wandered about, doing nothing in particular. She'd already slept in late and been given breakfast in bed. "I'm *OK*," she'd kept saying to Mum. "It was *Daisie* they kidnapped, remember? Not me."

She kept ringing Dita, but there was no reply. Maybe she and Inga had gone back to London with Liz.

Maybe Martin had gone, too. After all, he *was* Dita's dad.

She'd miss Dita, Becca realized. She was missing her right now. With Dita around, life seemed to explode. All night she'd dreamt about zooming around in a racing car and firing at crooks, and then she'd woken up to this grey afternoon that seemed to drag on for ever, to a kitchen smelling of chips and detergent and Mum's flowery cologne, and a DJ on the radio burbling on about birthdays.

The two old ladies came back from their trip to St Ives. They eyed Becca excitedly.

"You feeling better now, dear?" asked one. "What an ordeal!"

"Your mother told us all about it," said the second. "And we heard it on the radio. Shocking business. You're a very brave girl."

At six, Dad turned up, waving a paper. "Fame at last!" he announced, spreading it out.

MISSING GIRLS FOUND SAFE, said the headlines, and Becca saw pictures of Daisie and Dita.

Mum was turning on the telly when the phone rang.

Dad picked it up, then gave it to Becca.

"Hi," said Becca listlessly. Then: *"Daisie!"* she shrieked.

"Watch the news!" squeaked Daisie. "Go

on. Watch it. I'll you ring back."

Becca sat through the main news. She sat through the weather forecast.

Suddenly she saw her own face.

"Yuk!" she said. "Who gave them that awful school photo?"

"I did," confessed Mum. "The reporters came round this morning, while you were still asleep."

"An international kidnap plot," the newsreader was saying, "has been foiled by an actor from a summer touring company and this eleven-year-old girl from Tregennack – not to mention her dog."

"But Drac's *not* mine," corrected Becca.

"According to police reports," the newsreader went on, "Daisie Trevelyan, missing since Thursday, had been kidnapped by a gang who mistook her for Perdita Powell, daughter of Liz Powell, director of the BREAK-THROUGH chain of fashion shops. The two girls appear to be almost doubles. Daisie's now recovering in hospital from a massive dose of sedatives..." There was a shot of Daisie cuddling Drac in a room full of flowers. "We have not yet been able to speak to Daisie's friend, Rebecca Hughes, who seems to have led the rescue..."

Becca flushed pink. "But I didn't! It was Dita. It was Martin." Then she grinned. "It was really Drac!"

"A young Italian woman, wounded during the incident, is now in a serious but stable condition, and under police protection…"

Suddenly the newsreader's voice went solemn.

"The body of a man found on Carnaquidden Downs has been identified as that of Nicholas Sparrow, a representative of Guinevere Property Developments. The police are treating his death as suspicious…"

"Oh, no," whispered Becca.

The phone rang again. She picked it up.

"That man *killed* him." Daisie sounded shocked. "That man *killed* Tweetie Pie."

"We can't call him Tweetie Pie any more," said Becca. "It's not right. I mean, he's dead."

"He wasn't that bad," said Daisie.

"You didn't see him kicking Drac."

"I mean, nobody's that bad," said Daisie. "Well, maybe that man was…"

Becca fell silent. "Seen Dita?" she asked at last.

"This morning. At the hospital. Who do you think turned up with all those flowers?" She laughed. "They *all* came. The nurses nearly flipped!"

"Who came?"

"Martin, Perdita, Inga, Mum and Dad and Ben." Daisie was breathless. "And Liz."

"You mean, Dita's mum?"

"I said Liz," repeated Daisie. "Listen, my

worm – you haven't *seen* her!"

Reporters pestered them again on Tuesday.

Mum bustled about in her Parents' Day dress. "Ten minutes only," she told them. "My daughter's still under stress."

Becca told her story over and over. "It was really Drac who did it... That's right, Dracula... No, he's *Daisie's* dog. Her brother likes vampire films..."

On Wednesday afternoon, they walked over to the Trevelyans.

Ben opened the front door. "If you're Press," he said importantly, holding Drac by the collar, "then get lost." Drac whined, then wriggled free. "Well, that's what Mum's been telling them." He grinned toothily. "Hi, Becca. Hi, Mrs Hughes."

Daisie pushed out past him, followed by Dita. She gave Becca a bear hug. "You were the greatest," she said.

In the kitchen, a slim, spiky-haired woman in a splashy print dress was stubbing out most of a cigarette. "You see?" The woman winked at Daisie. "She's really bossy, your mum."

Daisie's mum shrugged. "I told her – one cigarette in my house and that's your lot. Then she started on a second."

"Not good for you, Mrs Powell," said Inga. "I tell you before. I give them up long ago. Not cool in Sweden."

Liz sighed. "Cigarettes help me unwind," she explained. "In my business, you have to do *something*." She turned to Daisie's mum. "Fancy a job as my personal masseuse? I'm serious." She began pulling out another cigarette, then pushed it back in. "If you can make me feel as relaxed as this after what's happened in the last few days..." Her hair glinted bronze in the afternoon sunlight. "Rent your house, Joanna," she said. "Come back with us. You need the money and Daisie could go to school with Dita." She laughed. "It would be so amusing. People will think they're twins!"

"They look like twins," said Becca's mum. "I'd never have believed it."

Becca groaned. "I *did* tell you, Mum," she said.

Liz's voice grew husky. "I owe you all so much. I'd like to do something for you..."

"Oh, *please,* Mum," begged Daisie.

"Out of the question," said Daisie's mum. "What about Ben? And the animals?" She reached for the kitten who was playing with her hair. "And what about my work here? And what about Daisie's dad?" She set the kitten gently on the floor and it scampered away. "Anyway, it's Becca we should both thank," she said. "And what about your own girl?"

Dita suddenly looked furious. "You're all

129

forgetting about Martin. It was Martin who took all the risks. It was Martin who got hold of that woman's gun." She glared at Liz. "It's Dad you should be thanking."

"Don't you think I know that?" Liz stared hard at the floor. "And don't you think I have?"

"She's hatching something," said Perdita. The three girls were sitting on the beach. "They're all hatching something."

"Who do you mean?" asked Daisie.

"Liz and Inga. And Dad." Dita sighed. "Liz goes all soppy every time we mention his name now – the way she looks when she's thinking about a new boyfriend." She giggled. "Maybe they'll get married…"

"Aren't they already?" asked Becca.

"Those two?" Dita looked astonished. "You must be joking! Anyway, he's a Fitzpatrick and she's a Powell." She pulled a face. "Perdita Fitzpatrick. Doesn't it sound awful?" Then she grinned. "We're a one-parent family, Liz and me."

"But don't you want them to get back together?" asked Becca.

"Don't know, really." Dita sighed. "They're so *different*. They'd only fight, just like they used to."

Becca thought of her own peaceable dad. She couldn't imagine him having a row with her mum.

"I'd like to see more of my dad, though…" Dita sifted small pebbles through her fingers. "And it would be great if Liz stopped putting him down."

"Well, she can't do that any more," said Daisie. "Martin was a hero. Or so the lot of you tell me. I can't remember." She went suddenly quiet. "Poor old Tweetie Pie."

"What really happened?" asked Becca. "How did he get you in the first place?"

Daisie looked embarrassed. "Ice-cream," she confessed. "I was coming out of the pasty shop and Tweetie Pie was waiting in the van. Called me Perdita. Asked if I'd fancy one of those Cornish Cream Specials again."

"Gutsy!" teased Becca.

"And then that woman turned up. I thought she was his new girlfriend. I mean, he went for foreign accents – remember his thing about Inga? Well, she bought us strawberry milk shakes…"

"Pig!" exclaimed Becca.

"And then, at the end, she offered me a lift home."

"You mean, to my place?" said Dita.

Daisie nodded. "I was going to bring her in, and surprise Inga. Then she stuck that needle into my arm…"

Becca shuddered. "Ugh!"

"That man must have paid Tweetie Pie a bomb, though," said Dita. She shook her

131

head. "Poor old Tweetie Pie. He didn't know who he was playing with."

"Who *was* he playing with?" asked Becca.

Dita shrugged. "The Mafia, maybe. Or something like it…" She paused. "Mum gave in to them, you know. Cancelled all those shops in Switzerland."

"She gave in?" Daisie was horrified. "But that's awful! They'll go and do it to someone else."

"Liz didn't see it that way." Dita fiddled with a shell. "Said her family mattered more than any old business deal. I mean, what would your mum have done?"

Daisie looked bothered. "Well, if they'd got Ben, I suppose…"

"Mine would have given in too," said Becca.

They sat, deep in thought.

"Anyway," announced Dita. "You've all got to come round to my place on Saturday at four."

"Why?" asked Daisie.

"Ah…" Dita grinned. "How would I know, my worm?"

CHAPTER
NINETEEN

The little car park was already crowded by the time Becca's lot turned up on Saturday.

"Oh, look!" Becca pointed. "There's Martin's car."

And next to a BMW stood the Topsy-Turvey Theatre lorry, with painted moons and stars and glittery letters.

"Couldn't miss that lot," sniffed Mum, "if you tried." She smoothed down her dress and patted her hair. "And isn't this van from that new ice-cream parlour?"

They walked around, looking. "There's the pies and pasties shop," said Dad, peering. "And the St Austell Fruit Farm lorry." He grinned at Becca. "Your friends running a supermarket?"

They went down to Dita's house but there was no one around.

"They're all on the beach," gasped Becca. "Look!"

There were two trestle tables looped with tissue paper garlands, and the most wonderful picnic Becca had ever seen. There were trifles and jellies and mounds of sugared strawberries. There were pasties, pies and sausages, and big bowls of crisps.

Liz appeared, in a gold bikini top and long, flowered skirt. She put an arm around Becca, and smiled at Mum and Dad.

"You must be so proud of this daughter of yours," she said, and Mum went suddenly pink, and nodded, and squeaked, "Oh, yes, we are."

Then Martin came striding out of the crowd. Liz looked up at him adoringly.

"How's Supergirl?" he asked, tweaking Becca's hair. "And where's that dangerous dog of yours?"

"Drac's not mine." Becca was tired of saying it. "He's *Daisie's*."

"Who's Daisie's?" Daisie had come up to them. "Hi, my worm," she said to Becca. She fanned herself with her hand. "I'm baking," she announced. "Coming for a drink?"

Drac suddenly emerged, leaping and barking, followed by Ben in a red and black football shirt.

Martin tossed Drac a sausage.

"That dog'll be sick," said Daisie's mum, "before this party's over. Just you mark my words."

"Sorry," said Martin. Then he gave a little

cough. "Will you excuse us?" he said to Becca's mum and dad. "I think Liz wants another word with Joanna…" and Daisie's mum put on one of her special, knowing smiles.

Daisie watched them moving off, talking, arguing. "That lot are up to something," she said to Becca. "But what?" She went over to the drinks table and picked up two iced lemonades. "Cheers, my handsome!" she said, glugging hers down.

Perdita appeared in a swimsuit and flip-flops. "Brought your swimmers?" she asked. "Bet you didn't. Never mind," she added when the two girls shook their heads. "You can borrow some of mine. I always pack too many."

They went back to the house to change, then ran down towards the sea.

"Your lot and my lot are up to something," puffed Daisie.

Dita grinned. "I know," she yelled.

"Then tell us," threatened Daisie. "Or you'll get ducked!"

They dumped their towels on the sand, then splashed into the shallows.

Daisie started a water battle. "Go on, tell us!" she said.

Dita eased herself on to a moss-covered rock. "OK, OK…" She flicked water at them with her toes. "It's some big old barn outside Tregennack. Liz wants to buy it."

Becca burst out laughing. "She must be half daft! She can't sell clothes like that in Tregennack!"

"It's not clothes." Dita was looking smug. "Liz wants to turn it into a health centre and she wants Daisie's dad to do the conversion..."

"Wow!" breathed Daisie. "So he'd be home with us again!"

"...and she wants Daisie's mum to do her massage stuff, and herbs and vitamins and things. So we'd have to *live* down here." Dita was breathless. "At least part of the time. And Dad's company tours Cornwall every summer..." She slid into the sea and came up shaking her head. "You know, your mum's really got to her!" she said to Daisie.

"Oh, Mum's so bossy," sighed Daisie, floating on her back.

They towelled themselves dry and ran back to the feast. They ate, they splashed around, then they ate some more.

"I'm up to here," gasped Daisie, flopping on to the pebbles.

"Another ice-cream?" teased Becca.

Daisie groaned. "I don't want to *know!*"

Inga came over with two press photographers. "Be quick," she said sternly. "This is private party." She stood, looking down at Daisie and Dita. "Like two twins," she muttered, shaking her big flower earrings. "I still not believe..."

The girls went up to the house and changed back into their clothes. Dita picked up a dress and offered it to Daisie. "Put this on," she giggled. "See if we can fool Liz!"

The theatre people began putting up a structure on the beach. They made up a platform out of trestles and boards.

A rocket suddenly swooshed against a mauve and orange sunset.

"O-o-oh!" people gasped, and, "A-a-ah!"

Martin coughed deafeningly into a mike. "It takes something like that to shut you lot up," he joked. He cleared his throat dramatically. "I have some announcements to make. We are, as you all know, celebrating the safe return of Daisie Trevelyan, not to mention her amazing look-alike friend."

And everyone clapped and cheered.

"You will be pleased to hear," Martin went on, "that a man was arrested this morning at Southampton Docks."

They cheered again.

"The police had built up a great Photofit picture of him from Daisie's descriptions…"

"Daisie, Daisie," somebody sang out.

"I thought you were doped," said Becca.

Daisie grinned. "Not all of the time, my worm."

"Three cheers for Daisie!" called Becca's dad.

"Don't forget Becca," said Martin. "And

Perdita. And Drac." He smiled. "That dog solved the case single-handed."

"Don't you mean single-pawed, my handsome?" yelled Daisie.

When the noise had died down, Martin continued. "The man will be charged, among other things, with the murder of Nick Sparrow. And the attempted murder of his partner, Claudia Verdi."

There was a shocked silence. Then people began muttering.

"That man from those developers..."

"He was up to no good, was he?"

"Nick Sparrow wasn't really evil," went on Martin. "He was foolish. And greedy. And they offered him a fortune, not much of which he got... But there's bound to be some kind of enquiry. And in the meantime, work on Merlin's Hideaway will have to stop."

"And a good thing too," someone shouted.

"Time to organize a proper protest, then," said Martin, "if that's the way you feel."

And people clapped again and cheered.

"It's all right for you lot," grumbled Daisie. "But I wanted to go to London."

"But you can," Dita told her. "And Becca can, too." She sighed happily. "It'll work out. I know it will. Everything will work out," she said. "You'll see."

Suddenly fairy lights came on around the platform and three fiddlers in clown costumes climbed up to play. And by the time the first star came out, everyone was dancing.

Even Drac.

THE TIME TREE

Enid Richemont

It was extraordinary.
Suddenly someone was there and it wasn't Joanna. Someone was helping, holding Rachel, guiding her down. Rachel caught a glimpse of curly brown hair fringing a white lace cap...

Rachel and Joanna are best friends and the tall tree in the park is their special place. It's Anne's too. So it hardly seems surprising that the three girls meet up there – except for the fact that four centuries divide their lives.

"Ms Richemont develops her story beautifully, with finely controlled writing and clear delineation of her three main characters." *The Junior Bookshelf*

PIGEON SUMMER

Ann Turnbull

And then she was there!
Speedwell – it had to be her!

The year is 1930. Eleven-year-old Mary
Dyer loves helping her father look after his
racing pigeons – much to her mother's
disapproval. Ruby, Lenin, the Gaffer –
Mary has names for all the birds,
including her favourite, the aptly named
Speedwell. When her father has to leave
home in search of work, Mary takes on
responsibility for the pigeons. But during
the difficult summer that follows, she and
her mother find themselves in ever greater
conflict…

"A wonderfully moving story … I would
recommend it to anyone."
Sarah Whitley (12),
The Independent on Sunday

Shortlisted for the Smarties Book Prize

THE ROPE SCHOOL

Sam Llewellyn

"Far out there on the knife-cut rim of the world, a tiny sun winked and died...
Kate said, 'What—'
Jago turned. 'Breathe a word,' he said. 'One word. And I'll kill ye.'"

It's 1813 and England is at war with France and America. Entirely by accident, eleven-year-old Kate Griffiths finds herself at sea, disguised as a boy, in the Rope School of one of His Majesty's sloops of war. Under the watchful eye of the mysterious Jago, Kate learns about knots and sails, as well as the often harsh reality of shipboard life. But this is nothing to the tangle of intrigue and adventure that awaits her on the high seas!

MORE WALKER PAPERBACKS
For You to Enjoy

☐ 0-7445-1447-9   *The Time Tree*
by Enid Richemont   £2.99

☐ 0-7445-3081-4   *Pigeon Summer*
by Ann Turnbull   £3.50

☐ 0-7445-3647-2   *MapHead*
by Lesley Howarth   £3.99

☐ 0-7445-3681-2   *Granny*
by Anthony Horowitz   £3.99

☐ 0-7445-3663-4   *The Rope School*
by Sam Llewellyn   £3.99

☐ 0-7445-3657-X   *No Friend of Mine*
by Ann Turnbull   £3.99

☐ 0-7445-3694-4   *Ride on, Sister Vincent*
by Dyan Sheldon   £3.99

☐ 0-7445-3679-0   *The Boyfriend Trap*
by Mary Hooper   £3.99